Call from the Past

Rita Traut Kabeto

Rita Traut Kabeto

Call From the Past

kabetofandr@gmail.com
http://sites.google.com/site/ritatrautkabeto

Foreword

Often times, during the early nineteen-fifties in post-war Germany, I had to hide under my bed to read the book my sister Paula didn't want me to have. Belly down, I would slide across the waxed and polished linoleum floor underneath my bed, keeping my head down to avoid catching my hair on the springs that supported the mattress. Then I'd turn over on my back, pull up my knees and lay them down sideways toward the wall to deep my big feet from giving me away.

The heroine of "Papa's Boy" was a girl who lived at the end of the nineteenth century, whose mother had died in childbirth. Her father, not having any sons, allowed her to grow up like a boy until a maiden aunt convinced him that it was time to mold the boy into a girl. She was sent to boarding school in hopes of becoming a proper young lady, but instead, she turned boarding life upside-down with her untamed and uninhibited spirit.

Around that time, my eldest sister, Erna, finished a three-year business course in a boarding school in Venusbrunn, a small town amid wooded hills that provided lots of fresh air and healthy living. My parents had sent her because we were blessed with eight children and not enough floor space for all the beds. Hanfurt, my hometown, was crowded with refugees from Eastern regions and guest workers from Southern European countries. It was littered with the shells of town houses that were waiting to be rebuild, gaping bomb craters, rubble piles we had turned into athletic hurdles on our way to the bakery, or the swimming pool, or the garden by the railroad tracks.

My parents were planning to send another child. I had completed the required seventh grade, and "Papa's Boy" had given me a taste for adventure and fun. Venusbrunn. That's were I wanted to go. That's where I wanted to be.

Not until much later in my life did I begin to understand the subtle working of the Spirit.

Call From the Past

On a Monday night in late August I arrived in Venusbrunn for my first year at boarding school. I had come with Ursula, a third year student from my hometown, Hanfurt. It was a mild, tranquil summer night as we trudged the long way from the railroad station to the convent, each of us carrying a single suitcase that held all our belongings for the next four months. The long, winding blacktop road was deserted. A few streetlights among a row of ancient chestnut trees spread a soft, idyllic light.

When we came to Anwaltstrasse we turned left, passed several gardens on the left and a print shop on the right. Next came the boarding school with attached convent. Ursula stopped at a pair of massive, recessed wooden doors and pulled on a long rope that rang a bright bell inside the building. After a few moments a dark figure opened the door and let us in.

In the dim light of the entry I saw a very old nun who had a smile of such deep affection as my grandmothers might have had for me if they were still alive. She wore the most ridiculous looking outfit I had ever seen. Her headpiece was shaped like a roof, with the gable on top of her head, the slanted sides coming all the way down past her elbows. The outside of this roof was black, the inside white, and the whole contraption was attached to some other white stuff which encased her entire head except for the prunishly wrinkled space between eyebrows and chin. Across her chest was spread a large white cloth, and from there on down all was black.

"Gruess Gott—God's greetings," she said with a feeble voice. My stomach squirmed with embarrassment at this nauseating piousness; I was not used to this traditional

1

Bavarian "hello." She had her hands tucked into the opposite sleeves. "Erna?" she said, looking at me closely from behind her glasses as though she knew me but was not sure.

"No. I'm not Erna," I said and decided not to get angry because she couldn't know that she had insulted me. "Erna is my sister. I'm Stephanie."

Another nun showed up with a flutter and flourish of her headpiece. Sister Angela, that was her name, was smaller, much younger, with a smile that was intense. Her complexion was waxy white, her chin and nose long and pointed, and her thin lips were as colorless as her face. Another "Gruess Gott," - another turn of my stomach.

Her headgear flapping energetically, she led the way down a long wide corridor with closed doors on each side and an immaculately clean sandstone floor. An awesome silence permeated this place, a silence that felt calm, and peaceful, filled with order and contentment as if nothing vile or sinful had ever, or could ever gain a foothold there. A curious feeling of comfort suddenly came over me, a sensation of coming home after a long absence. I had no time to think about it, though. We climbed a wide wooden staircase to the second floor bedrooms. Ursula went to hers, Sister Angela took me to mine. Leaving the door open for some light from the hall, I could count eight beds of which seven were occupied. Sister helped me put a flat sheet on my mattress and a coverlet on the featherbed. Then we stowed the suitcase under my bed, and after waiting for me to finish in the toilet room she wished me good night and left me alone in the dark room with seven strangers.

I lay in bed, not able to sleep for a long time. The windows stood wide open, but there was no sound. No cars whizzed by as they did any time of day and night back in Hanfurt. No motorcycle crowd revved up after the late show. No string quartet played mushy music in the Cafe across the intersection. No American GIs yelled "Hey, Baby!" at pretty passers-by. And there were no couples promenading up and down the street, talking, laughing, their sounds carried on the evening breeze through my open bedroom window into my third floor life.

It was the silence that woke me up next morning. Surely, any minute now Venusbrunn would come alive with noise, like Hanfurt, where trucks would be pulling out on their daily routes, trains would spew crowds of rushing workers into the streets, motorcycles and cars would chase down their business pursuits at forty miles per hour through cobbled streets that were built during horse-and-buggy days. All I could hear were the vague sound of an occasional distant car.

When I sat up and looked around I caught sight of a pair of big black eyes. The eyes belonged to a small pale face in the bed beside mine. Noticing my stare, the small face disappeared under the featherbed. I thought she must be very shy. She turned out to be a lot more than that.

The other beds were heaped high with featherbeds and fat pillows with deep dimples made by girlish heads. My bed stood next to a tall window, and through it I could see a garden that was surrounded by a high stonewall on two sides and stretched out of sight on the third side. Beyond the garden and a few houses, the country sloped toward a wooded hill, one of four that surround the small town of Venusbrunn.

"Gruess Gott! Welcome to Venusbrunn," said a cheery voice. I looked toward the door and saw Sister Angela looking around with a prissy smile. Her thin, colorless lips drew a straight line across her waxy face. She went from bed to bed to make sure that everyone had heard.

"Yeah, yeah!" said a voice from a bed in the corner. "We're ecstatically happy to be in this dinky little town where there's nothing to do."

Sister Angela looked around the room once more,

her lips frozen in smile, and then she went out. One by one, my classmates crept out from under their featherbeds, yawning and stretching, eight pairs of eyes scrutinizing each other. When I looked at my neighbor again, her big black eyes vanished under the bedding again.

A moment later, a hand emerged, reached for a bundle of something that was lying beside her pillow and pulled it into the feathery depth. Something else was left leaning against her headboard. When I looked closer, I could distinguish a light brown stuffed dog with long black ears and a missing eye, and a large bunny, spread out flat on its tummy, with long floppy ears. The bunny might have once possessed a pure white, fluffy body, but time and sleep-ins had made it gray and stringy.

"Somebody pinch me! For a minute I thought I was in Kindergarten," said a petite brunette whose name was Mechtild. She was shaking her head at the menagerie in my neighbor's bed.

Our dorm room was entered through the washroom, which had two rows of five feet high walls with rows of basins attached on each side. I discovered that my bed neighbor was also my preening neighbor. She was a scrawny little thing with dark, stringy hair that made her small face appear very white. Her shoulders were narrow and bony and held up a slip that hung empty around her flat chest. She looked like she never got enough of anything: food, confidence, affection.

We washed faces and hands, combed our hair, brushed our teeth. Then it was back to the bedroom to finish dressing and make our beds. The little person, oblivious to our incredulous stares, pulled her bundle out and unwound it. From a ragged baby blanket emerged a little black teddy bear that had lost most of its substance, and a seal that was as gray as the stringy bunny. She rewrapped them carefully in the rag, and then sat them down lovingly between their sorry comrades against her

4

headboard. From somewhere came a snicker, then another, and pretty soon the entire room was filled with laughter. Sister Angela appeared in the door and shushed us into silence. Talking was forbidden. Sister Angela, her eyes lowered modestly and her fingers working a rosary, moved between washroom and dorm room to enforce it. Talking was forbidden outside the dining hall where we lined up for breakfast under Sister Angela's watchful eyes. Talking was forbidden as we entered and found our places at the tables: tenth graders by the windows, ninth graders by the door, eighth graders, all new, right under her nose.

The dining hall had three tall windows that faced Anwaltstrasse. The windows were set deep into a two foot wall, and under their deep window sills were built-in cabinets in which we kept our supplies of butter or margarine, and jam—which had to be brought from home—and whatever other goodies one might have brought along.

We lined up behind our chairs, and when all were present and the morning prayer had been said, we were allowed to sit. One girl from each of the four long tables was sent to the window with sliding doors that led to the kitchen, to fetch baskets of sliced bread and gray enameled pitchers of "coffee" that was brewed from roasted barley. Before we were allowed to eat, though, each girl in turn had to introduce herself to the whole assembly. And that's when I found out that the skittish little thing to my left had the same name as I, Stephanie. Somebody had the bright idea to call me Stef and the little person Steffi. In time we would become known as the Steffi Pair. Right now it was a bummer.

Before we were finished, Mother Superior showed up. She started her welcome speech with the traditional Bavarian "Gruess Gott." She talked like a drill sergeant whose job it is to make a mensch out of a misfit. I couldn't take my eyes off her remarkably ugly face with its lively

5

little mustache that twitched and shrugged and rose and sank with the contortions of her mouth. She stood tall and powerful like a man, her thumbs tucked into the wide belt over her broad middle. It was impossible to think of her as a woman, and my mind created a new category of human beings who exist somewhere in the realm between male and female but are neither.

Then Sister Fallada, second-in-command and belonging to that same category, had a few things to say while her beady little eyes shot darts from behind her glasses. She was short, and slight, and easily overlooked. She was just reading us the daily dos and don'ts - mostly don'ts - when Steffi, who was sitting at my left, let out a short loud laugh. All eyes turned in my direction as Steffi shrunk into a tiny heap beside me and out of sight of the nuns.

Sister Angela whispered something to Mother Superior who suddenly shouted, looking straight at me, "Stephanie Sauerling! I expect you to follow your sister Erna's example. She was a good student who never gave us any trouble." Folds of disapproval rippled along the deeply entrenched ruts across her forehead. I pointed to Steffi, but Steffi looked straight ahead, as if only her body were present while the rest of her was somewhere else and therefore not involved.

I didn't know what made me angrier, that Steffi got me in trouble or that I was expected to be a second Erna who had to be the meanest big sister there ever was.

Steffi was handy, though. I kicked at her with my left foot but hit the leg of her chair instead and hurt my toe. I tried pinching her with my right hand tugged underneath my left arm. But Steffi moved deftly out of my reach the way Erna always managed to do. I began to fume. I forgot that I wasn't dealing with Erna, forgot that next to nothing had happened, remembered that Erna always got away with things, and I swore I'd get Steffi on the way out.

6

The washbowl came around. It held warm water and a brush to clean off our silverware, which we then wrapped into our napkins and stored in table drawers, one at each place. We were barely finished when the school bell rang, and we were dismissed. Before I could get on my feet, though, Steffi jumped up, snug past me and headed for the door. I hurried after her, and just as I was about to grab her by the skirt she pulled out a chair in passing, then stopped long enough to watch me run right into it, knock it over and fall on top. The last I saw was a smirk on her face. I could have strangled her.

Some of the girls who had seen me crash into the chair stood with their hands over their mouths, trying to stop giggles and chuckles from erupting. Feeling like a clumsy fool I got up and rubbed my bruised ribs, which did nothing for my bruised ego. And nothing could soothe the rage that I felt at being denied justice once again. Steffi, who had unwittingly plopped into Erna's footsteps but had escaped to safety, would not get away with it, I vowed, as the stifled giggles and chuckles exploded into uncontrollable laughter.

But she did. One look at me, and Steffi went dashing into the restroom, or hiding behind a nun, or weaving in and out of a pack of girls. After a time, this maddening chase began to feel pretty silly. I decided to ignore her.

Our eighth grade class consisted of fifteen girls from town and six boarding students besides Steffi and me. Mechtild, the petite brunette, was witty and very sure of herself. She had the same family name as a well-known Communist dictator, and she told me that this Communist was her uncle. Not knowing any better, and delighted to have such an important tid-bit of information, I eagerly spread the word. The nuns still suffered from the Nazi-jitters, which was compounded by fear of the American occupation forces and dread of the Bolsheviks. They were not amused to hear about this Communist connection, and the incident set the convent a-buzz like a hornet in a beehive.

Mechtild brought along a shadow all the way from home: big, homely, and boring Marlies who had a bosom the size of my mother's. Having no original thoughts of her own, she copied everything that Mechtild did and every new outfit that Mechtild wore.

Gusti was the oldest, most experienced, and most knowledgeable in all the tantalizingly forbidden subjects. On discovering that she knew what I didn't know, she agreed to teach me. What I learned, crouched on the cold hard floor in front of her bed one evening, filled me with such a mix of disgust and wonder and shame that I vowed I would never do that.

"Some day, when you're older and you meet the right man, you won't feel that way," she said. I decided to keep an open mind.

Roswitha, from the city of Nuernberg, sophisticated and ambitious, more often than not had her nose stuck in a textbook. Later, when even the nuns thought that it was too much of a good thing, she would smuggle them into the toilet room.

Then there was Helga, a war orphan who was living with a crotchety old maid. Helga's favorite escape phantasy was to live with her married sister in Berlin. But Berlin was divided, and all of it situated inside East Germany behind the Iron Curtain. She might as well have wished to live on the moon.

Ellen was a happy, cheerful sort with bad breath, which seemed to escape her notice. She had survived the siege of the Warsaw Ghetto, but fleeing before the upheavals of war in Europe had cost the life of her brother and given her a severe case of asthma.

Sister Hippolita, our eighth grade teacher and a marvel of a storyteller, was short and broad, her body above the waist shrunken and lumpy. She had a broad face and a complexion that was smooth as a baby's behind. Her rosy, fleshy cheeks nearly drowned a pair of lively little eyes full of sparkle and shine.

During study time, Steffi did it again. Sister Hippo had given her the seat directly in front of me. Suddenly, Steffi burst out in loud laughter. Quickly, she clapped her hand over her mouth and shrank down into her seat and out of sight. All eyes were on me again. Ah, the disadvantages of being born into a family of tall bodies, broad shoulders, long arms, and big feet!

"I didn't do that!" I protested, pointing toward Steffi.

"Stephanie Sauerling, this is study time!" Sister Hippo said, and the twinkle was missing from her eyes.

"Yeah, right," I mumbled and slouched down in my seat to escape being scrutinized by eight pairs of eyes.

When it felt safe to emerge again, I took my ruler and conked Steffi on the head. She let out a wail and her hand flew up to grab her head. Before I could feel a sense of satisfaction, though, someone nearly ripped the braids out of my head. When I turned around to see who it was, several frowns gave me to understand that I had become the villain.

"You're going to get it tonight," I hissed in Steffi's ear.

She stayed out of my way in the attic where we kept our clothes. She hung around Sister Angela during free time and during night prayer in the chapel. She even managed to ignore me from her bed.

"Why are you doing this to me?" I asked as quietly as I could and still be heard across the space between our two beds. Steffi turned her back to me and remained silent. I walked around her bed to the other side and repeated my question louder, but Steffi turned over again and, like a snail, pulled herself into her feather housing. The other girls went "shhhh" and "quieeeet", and that's when Sister Angela walked in, just when I had my angry arm deep inside Steffi's bedding to pinch a reaction out of her. With a look of embarrassment, Sister pointed to my bed. I went and said nothing.

I was furious. I lay on my back, my arms crossed under my head, thinking, figuring, guessing at Steffi's behavior, hitting my featherbed in sheer exasperation. The full moon stood above the woods, intensely yellow and bright, and its light flooded our room. After a while, I heard Steffi emerging from her bunker. I kept quiet. Suddenly, she let out a scream. Raising up and turning toward her bed, I could just see her disappear again.

"What's the big idea?" someone yelled.

Sister Angela appeared in the door. "What is going on here?" she demanded to know, and her voice was very firm this time.

"Oh, Stef is trying to make an impression," Gusti said.

"Hey, I didn't do that," I protested. Looking and pointing to Steffi's bed, which was flooded by moonlight, I opened my mouth to tell all. But a pair of black eyes, peeking out from under the covers beside a bundle of little faces, looked at me with dire pleading. The sight of it was so sad and so funny that it thoroughly befuddled me. Sister Angela left with another reprimand for me.

That was all I needed. I picked up one of Steffi's little creatures and threw it. Steffi bounced out of bed as if stung by a tarantula. "Henry!" she wailed and raised her arms for it. Someone in the corner caught it, and suddenly it came flying back with great gusto and sailed straight out the open window.

"Henry!" Steffi yelled again, ran to the open window after it and nearly flung herself out. Sister Angela came in. Steffi pleaded with her to get Henry back, that she couldn't possibly sleep without him.

10

"I just hope he's not caught on the grape vine," Sister said, and shaking her head she went out the door, taking Steffi with her. The room erupted in laughter.

Sister Elisabeth, the energetic one who could create a draft just walking down the hall, took us blueberry picking the following day. Like a mother duck she forged ahead, expecting all her little ducklings to follow. Across the street from the convent, we came by a shabby little house. It was surrounded by a jungle of trees and shrubs and a few struggling flowers. Beside the house, just a few yards away, lay a pile of sticks and branches big enough to rival a king-size beaver lodge. The whole place was surrounded by a wobbly picket fence that seemed to stand up more from tradition than good repair.

Most of the girls had paired up except for Steffi who stuck to Sister like a burr does to hair. I walked alone at the rear. Near the shabby house, I noticed Steffi suddenly dashing to the other side of the street. With her head hanging low and her shoulders pulled up she looked like someone expecting to get hit over the head. She walked quickly, almost ran, not looking right or left, and she didn't cross over again until the house was well out of sight.

Sister led us through cobblestone streets that were crooked and narrow. They were lined with houses that leaned against each other and had settled, like people, into imperfect shapes. Near the edge of town, as we turned a corner, I got a sudden look at a building in full view. The sight was so startling that I stopped dead in my tracks. I knew that I had seen it before, but I also knew that I could not have seen it since I had never been in Venusbrunn before. The three-story building, old and abandoned, stood back from the street, tucked into a hollow that rose behind the building into the forest. A stream flowed beside it, and in my mind's eye I could see a mill wheel churning and dipping merrily into the flowing water. The building was older than any others I had seen. Most of its windowpanes were broken. Shutters hung by a single hinge or had fallen off altogether. Adobe, which filled the spaces between the timbers of the walls, had begun to crumble.

Suddenly, a feeling of deep sadness swept over me. It lasted only a moment, then it was gone. I stared and wondered, looked away, looked back at the old mill with a fresh mind, trying to recapture that first impression in hopes of jarring my memory. Yet memory was useless because I had never been to Venusbrunn.

The girls were disappearing around another bend and I hurried after them. My mind kept going back and forth, back and forth, trying to unravel the mystery. But the harder I tried the farther it slipped away from me.

Sister led us into the woods on Wolkmann mountain, the tallest and nearest of the four hills that surround Venusbrunn. Where the trees stood less dense, the ground was covered with low brush and wild flowers, and sunshine roused the rich smell of the forest floor and drowsied bird song and insect gnit-gnats.

Picking blueberries was a dreary chore, though. The berries were teeny-tiny, few, and far between, and they grew low to the ground. When I spotted a dense grove of pretty young firs I pushed my way into the trees and found a very secluded little clearing that was drenched in quiet sunshine. Sister would never know if it was my pail or someone else's that hadn't filled the big bucket.

Suddenly, a body raised up out of the tall grasses - it was Steffi.

"Well, well, well," I said, surprised and amused at the sight of this beautiful trap.

Steffi jumped up and looked for an escape. But suddenly, as though giving up the escape she sat down again. She wrapped her arms around her pulled-up knees and buried her face among her skinny arms and legs. I sat down near her and said, "you owe me an explanation."

12

No answer.

"You got me in trouble," I prodded.

No answer.

"I just got here, but already I have a bad reputation with the nuns because of you."

Steffi raised her head and stared straight ahead.

"What's your problem?"

Suddenly, she turned her face to me. Her big black eyes looked scared, but her mouth was set with determination. "Did you ever see or hear things that nobody else can see or hear?" She asked.

"What are you talking about?"

"You know, last night, when I yelled? I saw something awful happening. A car accident. Somebody got killed in a car accident."

"You saw that from your bed?"

"And yesterday, when I laughed when Sister Fallada talked to us? Well, a bunch of elves were running up and down the table collecting leftover food. They were so funny that I couldn't help myself."

"Elves? As in fairies?"

"And the shabby house near the convent?" Steffi talked fast, as if she were trying to spill it all before she lost her nerve. " Well, there is an awfully evil something about it. I can feel it. It actually hurts me." Steffi began to cry.

Confused by this unexpected outburst, spellbound by what she had said - I had no idea what she was talking about. I felt as though someone had just emptied my entire brain of everything familiar and had dumped in a whole bunch of strange new stuff. So new and different was this stuff that my brain didn't know what to do with it. Perhaps she had hallucinations. That was something I had heard of. Or maybe a heat stroke. Should I console her, or should I get her out of the sun, I wondered. Finally, I figured sympathy could never hurt, so I moved closer and put my arm around her.

That was all she needed. Now she sobbed uncontrollably. I could feel her narrow shoulders shaking with emotion and didn't know what to do or say. When Steffi had calmed down she pulled a handkerchief from her skirt pocket and dried her eyes. "It's just awful to see something bad happening to somebody and there's nothing I can do to stop it. And the worst of it is, nobody believes me."

"What about your parents? Don't they believe you?"

"They are the worst. They think I'm crazy. Do you know why I'm here? They think that a heavy dose of religion will get all this nonsense out of my head."

I sat and stared. Steffi sat and stared. "I had a lot of trouble in my other school because of it. And my grades were pretty bad. If I don't do any better here then I'm going to end up in the... " I was thinking loony bin - "they call it a sanatorium." Her tears flowed again.

"Oh, don't say that," I begged, feeling more stupid and helpless than I ever had in my life.

"My parents said so. Hallucinations! That's what everybody tells me."

"What do you think?"

"Well, I looked it up in the dictionary once, and part of it sounds like what I have, but part of it doesn't."

"Don't people with hallucinations do crazy or dangerous things? Isn't that why they end up in a sanatorium?"

"That's right. And I don't do dangerous things."

"Just slightly crazy ones," it slipped out of me with a sigh.

"I'm sorry I got you in trouble," Steffi said and looked at me with her big black eyes that begged forgiveness.

"Don't worry about it. I'm used to it. Between my big sisters and my little brothers I get blamed for all sorts of stuff. Must be hard for parents to figure out who's guilty

14

with eight kids around. I have three sisters and four brothers, you know. But tell me more about what you see."

And Steffi smiled for the first time.

Spirits, she said she saw, and gnomes, and fairies. She looked like a fairy herself with those big soulful eyes framed by long dark lashes, shimmering with the remnants of tears, and a sad little mouth with droopy corners. Not only did she see Spirits, she talked to them and they talked to her. "They're the only friends I have. I could never tell anybody about them," she whispered, not looking at me.

I felt a tug somewhere inside. I wished she hadn't told me, though. It would have been simpler to just keep hating her. By lending a sympathetic ear I had become her confidant, even a sort of accomplice. I couldn't say anymore that I didn't believe her. It would have been too cruel. So I was stuck with at least pretending that I thought she was normal.

To think that there was more to life than people and animals was pretty fascinating, though. Once Steffi felt free to be herself, she turned out to be a great entertainer. And some of the antics she related of fairies and gnomes were hilarious. We completely forgot about blueberries and the world, sitting and talking in our little hiding place among the fir trees.

"Oh my goodness! What time is it?" Steffi suddenly yelled as she jumped up. Neither one of us had a watch. We dug our way through the trees in a hurry, but the girls were gone. We headed down the mountain as fast as we could.

We were late. Old Sister Regard with her perennial smile of blissful ignorance opened the door. Sister Angela came rushing toward us with flapping headgear. Explaining to her that we had done nothing but talk did not prevent a meeting with Mother Superior in the reception room. It was a small room that smelled of mothballs and stale air. Its ancient furniture was black, and stiff, and hard. Even the upholstered chairs were hard; I figured they were meant to last forever.

Steffi sat at the edge of her chair, her head pulled down into her shoulders, looking around the room as though it was about to execute her. When the door opened and Mother Superior roared in Steffi nearly fell off her chair.

"What do I hear about you? You separated from the rest of the girls and got lost!" she half demanded, half accused, and her mustache bobbed up and down.

"We were sitting by some trees, talking," I explained meekly. "I guess we didn't notice when the others left."

"How is that possible?"

"I really can't explain it." Then an idea hit me, and with greater courage I said, "I even wonder why the others left without us. Shouldn't they have waited for us, or called us?"

"Yes, I suppose they should have," admitted Mother Superior. "I will talk with Sister Elisabeth about it. But next time, see that you don't get separated. You hear? I would not want to report something like this to your parents. Now go to your studies."

Once back in the hallway, Steffi and I ran for our classroom, grinning at each other with the delight of shared secrets.

Saturdays were meant for confession. Our house priest, long past retirement age, lived with his housekeeper sister in the Villa, a separate building between the service buildings and the convent garden. He was a small, quiet man, wrinkled and hunched, who took great care and much time to affect the clear pronunciation of the sacred words of the Eucharist. One day, on Ellen's coaxing, I would ask him if French kissing by a cousin was a sin. Expecting a simple yes or no, I was not prepared for all the words this quiet little man heaped on me. I had no choice but to walk meekly by his side as he made seemingly never-ending rounds of the garden paths. I never did know what the answer was, and I never asked advise for someone else again.

Those of us who wanted to go to confession in town rather than meeting with our house priest face to face in the back of the chapel were allowed to do so without watchdog or chaperone. Three hours of unsupervised, uninhibited, unstructured free time! The nuns were pleased with the great number of penitent girls who rushed off to confession.

Susie and Gertrud, two of the tenth-graders, were making their confessions at the street corner without the help of a priest. Steffi and I saw them talking to boys, from the window of Café Pole where Steffi filled my mind with fairy stories while I filled my stomach with pastries.

"They're pretty stupid, standing there like that for the whole world to see."

"Hey! There goes Ellen. Do you think she'll tell?"

"It's the townspeople I'd be worried about. They have eyes and ears everywhere."

"How do you know?"

"My sister Erna. She had a girl friend who had a boyfriend here in town. Boys are taboo, you know. For the nuns, the opposite sex exists only in the form of fathers, maybe brothers, but never boyfriends. "

It didn't matter much that Steffi and I had decided not to tell. Venusbrunn had a grapevine quicker than telephone. As soon as we got back to the convent—Steffi keeping well away from the beaver lodge with a police car parked in front —Sister Angela took us to the courtroom again. Mother Superior stormed in. "What were you doing in town today?" she asked.

"We went to confession," I lied beside a frozen Steffi.

"No, you did not," Mother Superior insisted. I was

17

trying to decide whether it was safer to stick to my lie or come out with the truth when she shouted, "you have been seen talking to boys."

"That wasn't us," I blurted out with righteous indignation.

"You have been seen," she repeated, testing the strength of my denial.

"Well, I'm sorry, but whoever saw us, saw wrong."

"You are being disrespectful."

"Sorry," I mumbled.

After a moment of silence, she said, "you can go now. But be warned: if I ever find out that you fraternize with young men your parents will hear about it." She stormed out with such vigor that it seemed to suck the air right out of the room.

We giggled with relief as we ran to the classroom. Sister Hippo was not around yet. Remembering the police car, we went to a window from which we could see the old house. We were just in time to see a policeman shutting the wobbly garden gate.

"There is something evil about that house," said Steffi. "Look, even on a bright day like today, with nothing but blue sky, there is a big ugly black cloud hanging over the house."

"I don't see any cloud," said Ellen in passing, went to her seat and sat down.

"Hey! This is a private conversation!"

"Well, then hang a sign around your neck so we all know," she said and laughed good-naturedly.

"It's not a weather cloud," Steffi whispered. It's more like a blotch of ugly, dirty color. Everything has color around it, you know. Yours is nice and bright, but that blotch is real yucky looking, and I know that it means something bad." Sister Hippo came in, and her eyes twinkled us back to our seats.

After dinner, we asked Sister Angela what she knew

18

about our neighbor.

"Herr Mueller lives there. He's a fine old gentleman. Always polite and friendly," she said with a smile of enchantment, the kind that lit up my mother's face when in the company of someone important, such as our parish pastor; he owned two doctorates.

"Does he have a wife?"

"His wife died a long time ago," Sister said. Steffi looked at me as though she was on to something.

"How did she die?"

"She visited a relative during the last year of the war. The relative's house was destroyed in an air raid and they were all killed. He has been a recluse ever since then. Keeps pretty much to himself now. He doesn't seem to have any relatives, either. Poor man."

"I wonder why the police went to see him today?" Steffi said.

"Did they? Oh, I don't know. I hope he's all right."

Sister Angela taught shorthand and typing, and Roswitha, the nerd, had a question about our assignment. Then Sister had to shush Helga, Mechtild and Marlies who were laughing too loud about dirty jokes, which Mechtild learned from the butchers in her father's meat market. Gusti was more careful about such titillating subjects; she only talked in whispers about the anatomical aspects of sexual relations.

Ellen sat near us, and when her bad breath became too annoying, we moved a few chairs away.

"So, what do you think?" I asked Steffi.

"I don't know. All I know is that yucky cloud over his house."

"Maybe we should find out what it means."

"It means something evil, I told you."

"Yes, but what exactly? Did he do something evil? Is he hiding something evil? The nuns think we're evil for talking with boys. Is that what the old man is guilty of?

19

Talking to women?"

"Of course not, silly," Steffi said and laughed.

"I want to find out what evil thing the old man did," I said, looking squarely at Steffi.

"Good luck," she said, avoiding my stare.

"Where's Susie?" Someone yelled. "Isn't she going to play?" We were gathered at the blacktop to play dodge ball, and Susie was star player.

"Somebody snitched on her. She's got house arrest, and Gertrud too," said Martha, another 10th grader. Steffi and I looked at each other. A silent 'Ellen?' jumped like a spark between us. We looked to Ellen who stood in the crowd waiting to be picked for a team. She looked innocent enough.

"All right, let's get going," Marianne called. With Susie and Gertrud out of the game, my status as player, I figured, would improve. No such luck. Once again, I was picked last.

Whoommp! Marianne caught the heavy ball against her chest. She was built like a guy: broad, stocky and muscular. Her breasts, if she had any, had to be all muscle. After a few throws, Steffi was out. Another throw, and I was out.

"You're out," yelled Ellen who had thrown the ball that I couldn't dodge.

"Yeah, yeah, I know. You don't need to rub it in." I could have kicked myself for being so stupid. It was always the same thing: I could see the ball coming, kept my eye on it, but no matter which way I jumped, it hit me anyway. Steffi didn't seem to care. She was waiting for me on the bench under the Linden tree where the park and the blacktop meet.

Steffi had been daydreaming again. That's what Sister Hippo accused her of. Steffi told me that she had been watching sun fairies sliding down the sunbeams that came in through the window. "They land with a thud on Sister's desk, and then they try to jump over her wrist or her pencil, back and forth, while she's writing. It's the funniest thing. And it's a lot more fun than bookkeeping and all that other stupid stuff. What do I want with it anyway. I'm going to be a singer."

"This is a business school. Don't you know?"

"No! My parents never told me. Oh, now I get it. My father wants me to work for him in his shop, that's why he sent me here."

Suddenly, she began to cry. I put my arm around her and waited. I began to wonder why my parents had granted my wish to come here. It was my mother's firm belief that granting wishes to children would spoil them. My parents had never asked me what I wanted to be or do, had never told me what kind of school this was or what I would learn here. Years later, my mother would justify their decision with the remark that attending business school would enable me to earn a living. What did I want? I didn't have a clue.

"What a mess!" Steffi sniffled. I had almost forgotten that she sat next to me. "If I behave myself and stay here at the school I'm going to end up doing boring stuff in a boring office. And if I don't behave myself I'll end up in the - sanatorium." She drew out the word the way a priss would show off French. Steffi dubbed her forehead with her forefinger and started sniffling again. "That's just wonderful! What am I going to do now?"

"We'll think of something," I said out loud, while thinking that I didn't have the foggiest notion. I realized that I had come to think of Steffi as perfectly normal. And why not. There were plenty of saints who could hear and see things that other people couldn't. Sure, Steffi was not a saint, but neither were the saints while they were on earth doing all that wonderful seeing and hearing. And Steffi seemed a lot more normal than the other girls who had nothing but guys, make-up and fashions in their heads.

We had started walking again, from the Linden tree to the little wrought-iron gate that marked the end of the park and the property. The wobbly gate sagged in its hinges and was chained to the fence post with a padlock. Half hidden by shrubs and vines and overshadowed by tall dark firs, it seemed like a leftover from a forgotten time. We turned, walked the short end of the park, turned again and walked the back length that bordered a neighboring property. The path ran parallel with and about ten feet from the fence that separated the two properties, and the space between the two was filled in with overgrown shrubs and vines over which towered a dense canopy of tree tops that made our little park very secluded.

We walked quietly for a while, arm-in-arm, in rhythm with our thoughts and each other. Suddenly, a powerful sensation came over me. It was so vivid and startling that I stopped dead in my tracks.

"What's the matter?" Steffi asked

"I don't know," I answered. I motioned her to be quiet. I started walking slowly, turning inward, calling up that sensation again, to feel it consciously, purposely in the hope of discovering where it came from and why. I noticed myself walking ever faster and feeling an overpowering need to find something that had been lost.

When we reached the Linden tree by the blacktop again I felt very tired, as though I had just worked hard on a difficult task. Yet the task remained unfinished, and solving it seemed to slip farther away the harder I tried to unravel the mystery.

"Are you alright?" Steffi asked and looked at me as if I had fainted. Then, the focus of her eyes changed. She seemed to be looking right through me, "your aura is different. What's bothering you?"

We sat down at the bench under the Linden tree, but I could not tell her what had happened because I lacked the words to describe it.

When coffee time drew near we headed back to the convent by a different way. Instead of walking through the garden with its rows of vegetables, berry bushes, tiny orchards, and lawns where the nuns spread their white laundry to bleach in the sun, we walked along the inside of the high stone wall that bordered the convent grounds along Anwaltstrasse. When we came by the wrought-iron truck gate near the service buildings we could see through the bars that a police car was parked outside the beaver lodge again.

"Could you find out what evil thing the old man did?" I said to Steffi.

"I could. But I wouldn't want to. It hurts me to come in contact with it."

"You mean, you feel pain if you walk by it?"

"I sure do. Even when I just think about it."

"That's too bad. I was thinking that we should try and find out just what it is that you have, or are. Then, if you understand it, and you can explain it to your parents, maybe even find a book about it, then they would have to believe you, wouldn't they?"

"You don't know my parents."

"But you have nothing to lose. You either work in your father's business, which you don't want, or you get shipped to the—sanatorium."

"That's about it."

"And you wouldn't have to hide from other people all the time. Must be hard keeping secrets, huh? It makes you so nervous."

"You can say that again," Steffi whined.

"And don't you want to know why you are that way? And what it all means?"

"You're right," Steffi said, and she seemed to grow bigger with courage and resolve.

"How about starting right now?" I nudged.

23

"Okay, I'll start with the stick pile. Right now. Let's see if the washroom is open. I'll have a better view from there."

We were in luck. Sister Angela had forgotten to lock up the washroom, and nobody was around to see us go in. We stood at the window. "Hold my hand," Steffi said. She looked at the house, her face painfully contorted, squeezing my hand tightly. Then she closed her eyes and stood motionless. I held my breath while I held onto her hand. Finally, she said slowly, "I think there is a body buried under that pile of sticks..."

"Really?"

"...or two."

"Two of them?"

"I think so," she said and stepped away from the window, her face still showing signs of stress.

"Oh, my goodness," I whispered, too excited to know what to do with the information.

"Girls, what are you doing here?" Sister Angela's voice suddenly echoed through the empty washroom. "I will have to report this," she said, her mouth drawn into a prissy line across her waxy face.

"What have I got to lose?" Steffi whispered to me with a broad grin. Facing Mother Superior was not so bad this time. We took her tirade quietly. Even her facial antics were no longer entertaining.

Steffi seemed taller, more relaxed as we walked to our classroom. "Next thing to do," she said, "is to meet the old man face to face. Just do me one favor, Stef."

"What?"

"Talk me out of it," she whined, half laughing.

Susie and Gertrud were not allowed to go to town the following Saturday. The whys and wherefores were an open secret that Sister Angela refused to discuss.

"Let's meet the old man today," I said to Steffi on

24

the way back from town.

"Do we have to?" she said in her mousy way.

"Lost your courage again?"

"Well—no, not really.

"How about right now?" I said. "Come on, we'll pretend we're strangers, looking for an address. Like a number that doesn't exist."

"But you do the asking, okay?"

"All right. I don't mind. What's the worst that can happen?"

"He could bark at us."

"Right. And I'm used to it. So, come on."

By the time we reached the little house, Ellen, who had been to town alone, had caught up with us. We didn't need a snoop, especially one with bad breath. I stopped, pretending to retie my shoes.

"Knock, knock," Ellen, who had stopped with us, said to Steffi. Steffi backed off a step. "Who's there?" she said with a beleaguered look.

"Old man Mueller," Ellen said, laughed, and walked away.

"How, the heck...?" Steffi's words died in astonishment.

"Come on, we'll worry about it later," I said and headed for the door, afraid that Steffi might lose her courage. I rang the bell. After more than enough time for an old man to make it to the door, it opened slowly, as though it was stiff from lack of use.

"Now watch closely," I whispered to Steffi who stood behind me. I stepped aside, so that she would have a good look.

In the open door appeared an old man with a face that was lined with deep folds and had a complexion as gray as the hair on its head. His face was unshaven and his hair needed cutting. Food stained the front of his shirt and pants, his house slippers were worn. "What do you want?"

the old man said with a raspy voice and a suspicious look in his eyes. I felt Steffi's hands gripping my waist.

"Excuse me, could you please tell us where Anwaltstrasse 354 is?"

"There is no such number," he said and shut the door.

"Well?" I turned to ask Steffi.

But Steffi ran off and didn't stop till she got to the big convent door. "Oh, I don't like that old man. His color is just as black and dirty as the cloud I see over his house."

"Then he is the evil thing, right?"

"Right."

"Then, maybe the old man murdered somebody."

"Or two."

"And buried them in his yard. And to prevent anybody from snooping around...."

"Or dogs from digging them up…"

".... he piled the sticks on top."

Sister Regard opened the door and let us in. We headed for the dining room.

"You know what we should do? We should write down this information and give it to somebody to keep. Then, when we find out you were right, we have something to convince your parents with."

"That's a great idea! But how will anybody find out what he did?"

"I don't know yet. We'll have to think of something."

When we got to our classroom study time was about to begin. We pulled out paper and pencil and wrote down what Steffi had discovered.

Deciding whom to give the note to proved to be more difficult. Roswitha, we worried, would lose it among her stacks of books and papers. Ellen, the snoop—and perhaps snitch—was out. Mechtild and Marlies wouldn't take the matter seriously enough. Sister Hippo came in.

"Let's give each one a paper. Six, total," I whispered to the back of Steffi's head. Her head nodded.

Excitement over Herr Mueller's dead bodies made it hard to concentrate on such sober stuff as bookkeeping and business correspondence and shorthand. Sitting on a seat that didn't fit my bony butt made it much worse. Sister Hippo complained that I was fidgeting again. Explaining about the chair did not impress her, as though I was too dumb to know that my butt and the chair didn't connect. Thank goodness for the occasional trip to the toilet room.

During free time, that evening, we explained to the other girls what we had in mind. I explained, Steffi stood guard. They were to keep the sealed envelopes until such time that Steffi or I would give the go-ahead to open them. But we didn't know when it would be.

"Does it have anything to do with Herr Mueller?" Ellen asked.

"No it doesn't," I lied with heavy emphasis on no. Steffi shot me a worried look.

Marlies was afraid to arouse anyone's wrath and asked Mechtild what to do. Roswitha hemmed and hawed for a while. She certainly didn't want to get the nuns ticked off at her, guilty of too much study and not enough physical activity as she was. Ellen, with a knowing grin that made me feel very uneasy, thought it a lot of fun and agreed right away. Helga and Gusti could see no problem with it, so we got them all to agree. And to prevent anyone from forgetting where the envelope was placed they all put them in the bottoms of their night stand drawers.

After Sister Angela had left us for the night I whispered to Steffi who lay with her bundle in her arms, "now, let somebody say you're weird when that old man is found out."

"What do you mean?"

"We have to get that stick pile moved and the ground opened up, of course. How else are we going to prove that you knew something that nobody else knew."

"How the heck are we going to do that?"

"I don't know yet. We'll have to think of something."

"Shall we use one shovel or two?" Steffi asked a little snippy. I felt a chill.

"Well, we can't wait till he's dead, can we? That could take forever."

Steffi made a noise. I couldn't tell if it meant yes or no.

How to move the stick pile - that was the question. With a shovel? A rake? Piece by piece in the middle of the night?

"You have an appointment with Dr. Meyer today," Sister Angela said to me. October had brought a lot of rain, and I didn't look forward to trudging through the heavy downpour.

"What for?" I asked.

"A vitamin shot. Your parents requested it."

— A bulldozer would be so much faster —

Sister Eulalia, the nurse, went with me to Dr. Meyer's office. We saw her only when we were sick, otherwise, she stayed in the cloister, that very secret and secluded part where none of us students were ever allowed to go, not even the pastor from town who replaced our sick house priest one day. Instead of the chapel door, he made strides for the cloister door and put Sister Angela in a terrible dilemma because she had to stop him yet didn't dare contradict a priest. Flitting around him like a butterfly around a flower, she tried to tell him what she couldn't say. Not until he reached for the handle of the wrong door did Sister, in desperation and with her eyes lowered modestly, tell the priest that this door was off limits.

Sister Eulalia kept smiling at me as if she knew me as well as Sister Angela who read my father's letters to me

28

because I couldn't decipher his script, which was part Old German, part New German, part personal extravaganza. We had a long walk ahead of us, and by keeping five steps behind her I gave her to know that I couldn't stand her. It didn't stop her from smiling at me.

She was present in the exam room, sitting on a chair that the doctor had pulled over for her. She sat real close to me, with an eager smile on her face, like the one my aunt Emma always had on her face when she wanted to know what kind of underpants I was wearing. She'd wait till I was bent over the side of her balcony to watch my spit hit the sidewalk below, and then she'd lift my skirt to get a good look.

While the doctor got the needle ready, Sister told me to pull down my underpants. I refused. Sister insisted, but I kept refusing. Suddenly, Sister Eulalia reached to lift my skirt with one hand and to pull down my underpants with the other. "Hey!" I yelled, jumping back, scared and embarrassed. Sister said, smiling self-consciously, "come on, pull it down. Don't keep the doctor waiting."

"I can pull it up on the side," I said, and the doctor agreed that there was plenty of flesh for his needle. The eager smile vanished from Sister's face.

We were about to leave the office when I had a brilliant idea. "Can I ask you something?" I said to the doctor.

"Sure," he replied with the kind of smile that invites talk.

Sister Eulalia stayed put. "In private?" I whispered to the doctor.

"Sister would you please wait outside for a moment."

Sister was not pleased. But, like all nuns who believe that all educated men are infinitely wise, she left the room and shut the door.

"Doctor," I said. "What is it called when a person

can see things and hear things that other people can't?"

"The medical term would be hallucinations. Is that what you mean?"

"No, I don't think so. This person is perfectly normal." I noticed a look of amusement on his face. "Well, at least I think so. But she can see fairies and elves and she can talk with spirits. You know, all that stuff we read about in fairy tales."

"Oh, that! I think it's called clairvoyance."

"What is it?"

"I don't know very much about it. It seems to be a very special gift that some people have. Why some and not others, I don't know."

"Can you write it down for me?"

"Who is the lucky creature who can do all those wonderful things?" He asked, grabbed a piece of paper and wrote on it.

"Oh, I better not tell. Not yet, anyway. Maybe some day, okay?"

Dr. Meyer handed me the paper with the word spelled out on it. "Any time you want to talk, I'm here," he said.

"What did you talk to the doctor about?" Sister Eulalia asked, trying to disguise nosiness with sincere interest.

"Oh, women's stuff, you know," I answered, and that shut her up.

- We could remove a few sticks from the pile every Saturday -

"I know what you are," I nearly shouted at Steffi when I got back.

"What?"

"Stupid," Mechtild chirped.

"Shut up!"

"Clairvoyant," I whispered in Steffi's ear. "Let's check it out at the library Saturday." With that, I gave her

30

the paper.

"Hey, Steffi pair!" Mechtild said. "Cant' you talk a little louder? We can't hear you."

"What did you hear?" Steffi asked, looking worried.

"Enough," Mechtild teased, stretching the word in a singsongy tease.

"Sure you did," I said. I knew this little game; I had seven siblings. Poor Steffi was an only child.

— It would take an awfully long time to move the whole pile —

Ellen followed us to town on Saturday. To lose her, we walked through several winding, narrow streets that were covered in cobblestone and had no sidewalks. When we came to St. Kilian's Church we entered through the South door and after a few minutes left through the North door. We headed straight for the library.

The library was located in a charming old building at the periphery of the town square. City Hall, several shops, and an old Hotel enclosed the square on the other sides. I presented doctor Meyer's note to the librarian. With a look of puzzlement she took the note and went searching. Steffi and I followed her every move. But she could not produce anything on clairvoyance.

We left the library, wandered aimlessly through narrow, crooked streets, down the blacktop main street, which formed part of the old highway that connects Venusbrunn to Wallersheim in the East and Michelstadt in the West. There was little traffic in town except for a couple of bus loads of tourists who had come to see the old Abby church, a stately baroque sandstone structure with rococo interior and a famous organ. Afterward, they would go for a walk in the Seegarten and have coffee and pastries in the Seegarten Cafe.

Offices and most shops had closed shortly after noon. Housewives had purchased the roasts and sausages for their Sunday dinners and were at home, cleaning house and baking cakes and pastries for Sunday breakfast and afternoon coffee. I began to feel that strange sensation of loss again. I'd find myself walking faster and faster, Steffi complained that she couldn't keep up, and I felt as if the thing I was looking for could be found just around the corner, or the next, and I would surely find it if only I didn't give up. But it was all in vain.

When we came within sight of the library again, I had an idea. I motioned Steffi to follow me. She had given up trying to figure out where I was leading her. "Do you know the old man who lives across the street from the convent?" I asked the librarian.

"That's Herr Mueller you're talking about."

"What do you know about him?"

"I know that he has lived there for as long as I can remember, and I grew up here. I think he worked for the railroad. He was married, but his wife died a few years ago."

"Did he have any children?"

"No. Never did."

"Any relatives?"

"Not that I know of. But his wife was not from Venusbrunn. She might have had relatives somewhere else."

"Do you know how she died?"

"It seems to me, she had gone to visit somebody and died in an air raid. I think there was something about him in the paper recently."

"Really?" we shouted in unison.

"Oh yes, I remember now," she said. "A soldier—one of those that the Russians kept in prison camps for years after the war was over—he came looking for relatives. Frau Mueller was his aunt."

"The police car!" we nearly yelled, staring at each other, grinning from ear to ear.

"You want to know about it?"

"Yes, yes," I said, my insides all jiggly with excitement.

"Yesss!" Steffi squealed, her eyes big and bright with anticipation. A bad odor wafted by as we followed the librarian to a back room. Pointing to the piles and piles of dusty papers on countless shelves around the walls, she said: "Help yourself." With that, she left the room and shut the door.

"Good grief! Where do we start?" Steffi said.

"Find the one with the least amount of dust on it."

When we had found it, we sat down on the floor and started with the latest edition of the daily paper. I took one and Steffi took another. It was slow, tedious work. We read and searched and searched and read, and suddenly Steffi jumped up and shouted, "yikes! It's almost four!"

We had done it again. We came back late, and Sister Fallada's beady little eyes shot darts at us, and Sister Angela shook her head regretfully, and Mother Superior stormed and shouted. This time, she would write to our parents.

Punishment followed swiftly. We were not to go into town for a month of Saturdays. We could not be trusted anymore, Sister Angela said.

— An ad in the paper for free firewood should get rid of the stick pile really fast —

But the worst was yet to come.

Late that night, I got up to go to the toilet. Everyone seemed asleep; I moved very quietly. As I came around the basin wall in the washroom I nearly bumped into a warm body.

"Watch it!" said the startled body. In the moonlight I could see that it was Steffi. She stood by the open widow, her bundle in her arm. A mild autumn breeze rode in on the moonbeams. It was a lovely night.

"What are you doing here?" I asked.

"Talking to my Grandpa," she said.

Steffi was talking to her Grandpa! In the washroom of the convent! Why not! I could hear her closing the door to the bedroom as I opened the door to the hallway where I nearly ran into Sister Angela.

"Whom were you talking to?" she asked, looking past me to the open window.

I had to think fast. How much talking had she overheard? Steffi talking to her Grandpa? Or just the last few words between us?

"Nobody," I said.

She went to the open window and looked down to the street. "You talk, perhaps, to yourself?"

"That's right. Just me and myself. There is no rule against talking to myself, is there?"

"Don't be fresh. Go to bed now. We will deal with this in the morning."

"Can I pee first?"

"Being snotty will only make things worse. Go."

When I got back to bed, Steffi lay with her face toward me, dog, bunny and bundle lined up beside her on the pillow and taking up much space. It was a wonder she didn't roll out of bed.

"She's still outside," I whispered to her. "We'll talk tomorrow."

I couldn't stop thinking about Steffi's visit with her Grandpa. What a great opportunity to crack unsolved mysteries. Maybe he knew who the skeletons were under the stick pile. And maybe he knew who snitched on Susie and Gertrud. And how Ellen knew about Herr Mueller!

— Fire would get rid of the stick pile too —

Steffi filled me in at breakfast, which wasn't easy to do with so many ears around. Before she could finish, Sister Fallada came to haul me off to Superior Court. Steffi's anxious looks followed me to the door. Torn between speaking up and keeping quiet, her eyes were fidgeting in their sockets while her behind was fidgeting on her chair. I had told her not to worry. What could possibly happen. I had only talked. Big deal.

I nearly fell off the uncomfortable chair though, when I heard Mother Superior accuse me of fraternizing with boys. I could only deny it.

— Matches and paper would be pretty cumbersome for starting a fire —

I didn't know if she believed me or not until I got a nasty letter from my mother. Fraternizing with boys, fidgeting, being inattentive in class, being bored in chapel, disobeying rules, being a bad influence on others.... I was amazed at all the bad stuff I had committed, and it was only October. There was nothing for me to do; Mother would only believe the nuns. In my mind, nuns were indefinable shrouded beings, existing in a realm somewhere between male and female. In my mother's mind, nuns were representatives of God on earth. Since God is infallible, so must be his representatives.

— Gasoline would work much faster —

I was sent to the cellar to pick the white sprouts off the wrinkled old potatoes. The cellar was a dungeon; it had walls that were three feet thick, tiny windows that were blind from coal dust and age, and no more light than a dim bulb could spread. The familiar smell of mold and moisture reminded me of air raid shelters and bombings, cramped quarters, people covered in blood, but it roused no fear because I hadn't been old enough to understand.

I worked on the potatoes. I felt enormously proud of myself for submitting of my own free will to that which I didn't consider as inevitable. Feelings of calm purification flooded through me as I looked at the little pile that I had already cleared. That's when I noticed the slightest little movement in my hand. Looking closer, I saw that the potato I held was thickly covered with aphids. All the potatoes were thickly covered with aphids, and my bare hands had squashed and mangled all those horrid creatures and I could have screamed with disgust and revulsion. My head began to itch; I felt as if thousands of aphids were crawling all over me. That was more punishment than I deserved. I ran upstairs and beseeched Sister Fallada to let me off the hook. With a piously gloating smile she said softly, "offer it up to God."

Steffi picked one of the last roses from the convent garden that evening, pressed it between the pages of her favorite book, and gave it to me.

Not being able to get back to the library, I was stuck. Not helpless, though. We still had the girls from town who were ever so sympathetic to us for being locked away behind thick, high walls, for being separated from girl friends and boy friends, for missing out on dances and festivals, movies, and radio. Of course, fraternizing with the girls from town was also against the rules.

I had become friendly with Lotte. Lotte didn't know Herbert Mueller, but her brother, she told me, had a very good friend who lived behind the old man. She promised to bring us information.

— A friend from town could be playing with matches near the beaver lodge some night. There would be an unfortunate accident —

The information came two days later. Lotte pressed an envelope into my hand as she came into the classroom that morning. "What's that?" I asked.

"Just read it," she whispered and grinned mischievously.

Sister Hippo had not yet come in, so I hurried to the toilet where I could read in private. The letter was from Lotte's brother's friend, Willi. He wrote that he would give me all the information I wanted by the little gate in the back of the convent park. All I had to do was let him know when I could meet him there.

That was all I needed. Until now, I had been pretty innocent. If I went along, I would become guilty.

"I don't want you to do it," said Steffi when I told her about Willi. "I've gotten you in enough trouble already. Just forget the old man. It's not important."

"Hah! Now that things are getting exciting, I should drop the whole thing? No way!"

Before Lotte went home that day, I whispered to her, "tomorrow. 3:25, sharp."

I had pinned my braids across the top of my head to look and feel more grownup, but gravity wanted to pull them down.

"I better not play dodge ball today," I said to Steffi who was lined up with the others.

"What are you up to?" she asked. Her worried eyes searched my face. She had put on a few pounds since August, and with the extra body weight she seemed to have gained extra confidence. And Gusti, with a pair of scissors and a lot of talent, had worked a slight miracle on Steffi's hair. It hung in soft shiny waves down to her shoulders. With a couple of wings she'd be a pretty little fairy.

Ellen was staring at us so intensely that I feared she could see what we were thinking. I turned around and pulled Steffi along with me. "I'll wait for you on the bench," I said to her. A few throws later, Steffi was out.

She sat down beside me. "When it's time for coffee you go ahead. I'm going to meet Willi. And I think it's better if you stay out of this."

I had nothing to fear from my parents. They were only too glad to have a child or two away from home. It meant more space for the other seven and less stress for my mother. They would not bring me home for punishment. Steffi understood and left.

At the appointed time I stood near the wrought-iron gate at the short end of the park. I was nervous. I knew the girls would all be at coffee, but the nuns who were in charge of the grounds could show up at any moment in the convent's vegetables garden that bordered one long side of the park.

The sun shone warm and bright and turned garden and park into a palette of such glorious colors that the sight of it was overwhelming. The air was cool and a slight wind blew through my sweater. The wind swept up the leaves that were dry and brittle, swirled them into an eddy near the base of the grotto and dropped them, like a gift, at the feet of the Virgin Mary.

Willi showed up right on time. He was one cute guy! About seventeen, with straight blond hair that was combed back, blue eyes, and a crooked chin. He seemed to blush when he saw me, turning pink around the cheeks. Fresh and rosy like a baby, I thought. I love babies.

"Are you Willi?" I asked.

"Gruess Gott," he said and nodded. My insides squirmed with embarrassment. But his smile was so cute, and his teeth so perfect, and his eyes so blue, and—well, I decided to hang around.

"I hope nobody can see you out there," I said.

"Don't worry. It's a dead-end street," he answered in the local dialect, with a nice melodious voice.

"That's what you think. This town has eyes and ears everywhere."

"Yeah, I know," he admitted and grinned.

"So, what do you know about Herr Mueller?"

My eyes kept searching the garden for signs of flapping headgears while Willi told me that Frau Mueller had taken a train to Berlin, that she had died there, and that the old man had gone there for the funeral. He remembered the beginnings of the stick pile because he had asked the old man for some of the wood to build himself a tree house. The old man had said that he needed it, yet the pile had only grown bigger.

"The librarian said there was something about him

in the paper. Do you know what it is?"

"I don't read the paper. But I could ask my Dad. He reads everything."

"Yes, ask him, would you? I have to get going before somebody sees me here."

"Tomorrow? same time?"

"All right," I said, remembered to whisper "thanks", and ran all the way to the dining hall.

Steffi looked at me with her big eyes, trying to read my face. Sister Angela wondered why I was late. "Oh, problem in the bathroom; you know, women's stuff," I said, and she asked no more.

"Well?" Steffi whispered.

Noticing Ellen's eyes on me, I whispered back, "later."

Mother Superior showed up that evening. She told us that we would be able to go home for All Saints Day, a religious and legal holiday that was celebrated on November 1. For some of us, the trip might be too long to make it worthwhile. We should consult our parents.

She gave us some important hints for a safe train trip: never sit on a warm seat to avoid getting venereal disease. "What is venereal disease?" Steffi asked loudly. A collective gasp filled the room, then some giggles, then Mother Superior continued her instructions: beware of men. For an explanation, she read us a story about a girl who was lured by a man to his hotel room. She didn't know she had been lured until she saw the picture of a naked woman above the double bed. She saved herself just in time.

By the time Mother Superior was done, it was time for night prayer, which we said in the chapel. When prayer was over, the girls left but I stayed a while longer. The few candles on the altar threw a soft, flickering light. Five tall windows facing Anwaltstrasse were dark except for a little shine from a single streetlight. I loved the dark, and I didn't care what the Church implied about darkness and evil. For me, a victim of a ten-person household with one toilet and not enough floor space for all the beds, darkness meant privacy and seclusion, which gave me a chance to go inward and explore my thoughts and feelings. And did I ever need to explore my feelings! I had discovered that I liked Willi. A lot!

Once we were in bed and Sister had left, I took Steffi to the toilet and told her what had happened at the little gate.

"I don't think you should do it," she said.

"Don't you want to prove that you know what's under that stick pile?"

"Sure. But not if it gets you in trouble."

"So what. I've been in trouble before. I get in trouble without even trying. Might as well make it worthwhile."

"I hope Willi is worth it." She sighed with resignation.

Dressed in flannel nightgowns, side by side, we had our arms propped on the sill of the open widow that faced the garden. The wind had died down; the air was calm and cool. If I pushed my head and upper body way out I could pretend that there were no people or buildings, just woods and hills and stars in the night sky. The moon had come up over Beuchenberg. It stood big and round and seemed near enough to touch.

"Do you ever feel funny when the moon is like this?" Steffi asked.

"Funny?"

"Well, maybe not funny. More like sad."

"How come?"

"It's so beautiful that it makes me want to cry."

"Isn't it supposed to make you happy?"

"It does—at first. But the more I look, the sadder I get."

Suddenly, for just an instant, I understood. But

understanding was a slippery eel that zipped away before my mind could get a good grip on it.

We were quiet then, standing at the window with our heads and upper bodies pushed out as far as we could, bathing our faces in the light of the moon, which would journey slowly from East to West, shining into our bedroom, then the big girl's bedroom, then the washroom, and would start its rounds again the following night.

Sister Irmengard was fun. She had a bright, happy laughter. On our afternoon walks, she would pick apples off the trees that stood like sentinels alongside the road and stuff them inside her black robe which lay in deep folds over her chest, and made us promise not to tell. She definitely did not belong in the realm somewhere between male and female. Sister Irmengard had had a lover; we were sure of it. She was tall and slender and had a chin that shone as though she polished it with great care every day. Her face was covered with faint freckles that pointed to red hair. How she had ended up behind convent walls was a mystery that had us gnawing on it like a dog on its favorite bone.

"Why do you think she never married?" Steffi asked. We were walking at the rear, keeping plenty of insulating distance between us and the other girls.

"Maybe her lover was a soldier who never came back from the war. I wonder how long she waited for him."

"That's so romantic."

"I just don't understand how she can be so happy. Could your grandpa find out for us?"

"No. I wouldn't ask him something like that."

"Why not?"

"I don't know. It just doesn't seem right. Maybe because it isn't important. Or because we don't have to know. " She shrugged, then pointed to the base of a great fir tree and said, "oh, look! There's a troll."

Of course, I saw nothing. "Well, tell me, what's he doing?"

"He's carrying a bundle of wood, and he's taking it into his little house under the roots. Trolls are really pretty ugly."

It had rained that morning, and the moisture was still dripping off the trees and made us as wet as if it were still raining.

"I bet he would drown in a few rain drops," I said.

"No. He doesn't get wet at all."

"How come?"

"I don't know."

It was getting late and I was getting nervous about Willi getting there before me, and maybe not wanting to wait. I was walking ever faster, working my way to the front of the group, and Steffi had trouble keeping up. "How's my face?" I asked her. "Is that big pimple on my nose almost gone?"

"Yes, its' almost gone."

"But there's another one growing on your chin," Ellen said and laughed.

"And it's twice as big as the one on your nose," Mechtild added.

I looked at Steffi, but Steffi shook her head.

"Yeah, right," I said to Mechtild. "You should have boobs as big as that pimple." Steffi cracked up laughing.

I was the first one to make it to the door and rang the bell. I had to put away my coat first and get my apron. It substituted for a uniform—making everyone more or less equal.

"Hi!" I puffed, out of breath when I got to the gate.

"Gruess Gott," he said, and I didn't mind any more. His smile was so cute that I forgot for a moment what I had come for. I tried to keep a straight face, but I couldn't suppress an explosive smile that I felt spreading across my face that was probably as crooked as Willi's chin.

"My Dad knew about Herr Mueller. He said that the old man's wife has a nephew who came back from a Russian prisoner-of-war camp just last year. He is trying to find relatives."

"And his aunt is dead."

"Right."

"I wonder how we could get in touch with this guy."

"I don't know," said Willi. "But I could try."

"Gee, thanks a lot Willi. You're a real friend." I couldn't think of anything else to say, yet I didn't want Willi to leave. Willi's eyes moved this way and that, looked at me and past me, stared at the ground while the heel of his foot scraped away the fir needles that had piled up around the gate. His hands gripped the gateposts.

"And if you can figure out a way to get rid of the stick pile, let me know," I suddenly blurted out.

"What are you talking about?" he asked. His foot stopped scraping, his hands still gripped the posts, and it seemed to me that if the gate hadn't been there he would have gripped my hands instead. A hot wave washed over me and settled in my stomach.

"Did you ever wonder why that pile is there?"

"No, not really."

"Think about it! I mean, people around here spend a lot of time and effort to keep their yards neat and tidy. So why that pile of sticks? And it isn't even hidden out back somewhere but for the whole word to see and complain about."

"I'll think about it, I'll think about it," Willi agreed with a laugh and a slight move backward as though retreating before an onslaught. He said to give him three days to find out about Herr Mueller's nephew. I gave him five because we were going home for All Saints day.

"Good-bye, Willi," I whispered with my face close to the gate. Willi flashed his gorgeous smile with his perfect teeth and his heavenly blue eyes, and I never saw his crooked chin again.

Steffi and I went to the station with most of the other girls. The sidewalks were slick with wet, decomposing leaves. It drizzled a fine rain that soaked my cotton stockings and ran into my shoes. An even layer of thick gray covered the sky. "Do you have the word?" I asked her when her train pulled up. She took a piece of paper from her coat pocket and showed it to me.

"Don't forget to go to the library. I will, too."

"I will, too," Ellen piped up with a sly grin.

"Mind your own business," Steffi yelled at her. We moved out of earshot.

"I hope your parents won't be too mad at you, Stef."

"Don't worry about it. "

It was time to board the train. We hugged, Steffi climbed aboard with a sweet-sour smile. She came to the window to wave. Some of the other girls were waiting for a different train to travel in the opposite direction. Suddenly, Mechtild shouted, "you forgot your Teddy!" "And your seal!" Marlies added. A look of panic spread across Steffi's face. She turned to reach for her suitcase, but suddenly turned back to the window, shot Mechtild a dirty look, and then smiled with satisfaction at me. The train took off and Steffi waved till it vanished around a bend. My train came fifteen minutes later.

My mother didn't worry me too much. Because of All Saints Day, a Catholic and legal holiday, I knew she'd be preoccupied with a million things. All Saints Day was followed by All Souls Day — not a legal holiday, yet both days mandated attendance at mass if not by the Church then by Mother.

Mother was not a well-organized person. Not until the last minutes before store closure would she remember that one of the children needed new shoes or a coat. She'd be fussing about candles for the grave lantern, that had to be dug out of the attic and cleaned off, and matches that could never be found in our house; and buying enough groceries for the holiday; and the little kids would occupy her mind to no end; and the only clock in the house that worked but didn't keep good time would make everyone late for services. Father would be angry for being late for church and having to squeeze onto a skimpy bench behind the great pillar from where he could see nothing.

And that's just how it was.

November 2nd, All Souls Day, we went to mass again. Then, Mother had errands and grocery shopping for me to do, and that was my chance to go to the library.

I had walked past the State Library almost every day of my life yet had never thought to enter it. Housed in a modern, squarish building, it had never caught on in a town full of glorious Baroque architecture. With high hopes I approached the information desk to ask for books on clairvoyance. The librarian led me to a section that was labeled 'Esoterica.'

"That's not what I'm looking for," I dared to inform her.

"Nonetheless, this is the section that would have information on clairvoyance. Let me know if you need help."

"Thanks," I mumbled, overwhelmed by the number of books that waited to be examined. Of course, none of them were labeled clairvoyance. That would have been too easy. But I found a dictionary of esoteric terms, and there I found it explained very nicely. I could even understand it, or so I thought.

On the way home, my mind visited with Steffi. I tried to explain to her what I had learned, and that's when I discovered that I didn't have a clue. I had understood what the book said, but when I tried to put it in my own words - good grief!

By the time I had to pack for my return trip, Mother

felt bad for not having paid any special attention to me. She packed my suitcase with two sets of clean sheets, towels and washcloths, a few warm clothes, and she even sneaked in a brand new Western novel, a remarkable act for Mother who believed that giving gifts outside of birthdays and Christmas would spoil a child. Hired help would come the following Monday to wash the dirty laundry I had brought. Mother would return it to me by mail.

Father came upstairs from his downstairs office to give me his farewell speech. It was accompanied by a firm handshake, greetings to the nuns, and his usual "keep your distance." The meaning of that advice remained a mystery. Then he returned to his office. Mother shook my hand and kissed me and told me to obey the nuns. My sister Erna walked me to the station. "Say hello to Sister Irmengard," she said as she lifted my suitcase into the railroad car. She stood back, her forehead wrinkled and her eyebrows angled in a queer mix of question and doubt, and waited until my train was out of the station.

Since I had the farthest to go, I was the last one to return. The girls were all in bed; boisterous "hello's" and "hi's" and "God's greetings" ricocheted around the dorm room. With the hallway lighted and the door open, Sister Angela allowed us some time to settle down. Steffi waited patiently with her big black shining eyes on me.

"What did you find out?" I asked her, leaning out of my bed and she leaning out of her bed so that our heads were close.

"You will never believe what happened to me," she whispered. She had gone to several bookstores and had come to a particular little shop that had no books displayed in the window. She had thought it a waste of time to go in, but some inner voice had told her to go anyway. Before she could explain what she wanted, the shop owner said she had just what Steffi needed, went to a back room and returned with a book.

"What's the book about?" I aksed.

"It's called The Unseen World."

"How did she know what you wanted?"

"She held a little glass ball by a chain over the book , and the little ball swung back and forth, and that's how she knew what I came for, she said."

"But that doesn't make any sense."

"I know. So I asked her how that glass ball made her know. She said that it just helped her to focus, but that she got her information directly from Spirit."

"Spirit what?"

"I'm not sure. I think, she means Spirit like in Holy Spirit. Or life. Or God. I really don't know."

"Wow! That's powerful stuff!"

"What did you find out?"

"Not a thing."

"That's o.k. I think my book is going to tell us everything we want to know."

I laid back in bed and my thoughts drifted to Willi who would be waiting by the gate, rain or shine, and he would smile at me shyly, and dig his foot into the ground self-consciously, and just thinking about his eyes with their expression of something for which I had no words gripped me with powerful tension, and tears began to fill my eyes.

It poured liked crazy the next day, the day I was going to meet Willi. I ran to the little gate just long enough to tell him to meet me at Cafe Pole on Saturday at two p.m. House arrest was over.

"How did you get so wet?" asked Sister Angela when I came to coffee with my hair dripping, and all out of breath.

"I lost something in the park."

"What did you lose?"

"Oh, women stuff, you know," I replied, pretending embarrassment, and Sister asked no more.

That evening, Steffi and I attacked the book. It was very big, in small print, of fairly thin paper, and there wasn't a single picture in it. We read the words, but we didn't understand a thing. Every third word we had to look up in the dictionary, and some words weren't in it at all.

"Dang it," Steffi said and slammed the book shut in frustration. "Might as well toss it in the trash. It's totally useless."

"Maybe Sister Angela could help us."

"I know what she'll say." With her lips drawn tightly across her face in a prissy smile, she mimicked, "now, Stephanie dear, you must pay more attention to your studies if you want to be a successful secretary some day." It cracked me up.

"That's right, Stephanie, dear," Ellen, who sat nearby, mimicked Sister's prissy voice.

"Quit budding in, will you!"

"Shhhhhh," Sister Angela shushed from the far corner.

"That reminds me: How did she know that we were going to talk to Herr Mueller?"

"I don't have the foggiest notion."

"She must have super hearing."

"We better keep an eye on her."

Going to Cafe Pole the following Saturday, knowing that we were about to commit the ultimate crime, made me nervous. "Are you absolutely sure you want to be in on this?" I asked Steffi as we sat down at a little table in the back.

"Yes," she said, and she laid both arms on the table as if she were asserting her right to commit a blunder. Her voice was firm, and her head nodded rhythmically, punctuating her words, "I'm not doing anything bad; you're not doing anything bad. We're just talking to a boy. We just need some information. There's nothing wrong with that."

"What'll you have girls?" asked the waitress and

48

smiled warmly on us escapees. I ordered my favorite Black Forest Cherry Torte. Steffi only ordered a croissant. And we both ordered milk.

And then Willi came through the door. He looked ever so handsome in his blue corduroy knickers, plaid shirt, and heavy fisherman sweater. He looked around, spotted us in the back, and then headed in our direction. His eyes were fixed on me and caused my face to break out in a huge grin. I tried to squelch the grin, but it was hopeless.

"Isn't he the cutest thing?" I whispered to Steffi.

"He's got a crooked chin," she whispered back.

My elbow jabbed her ribs.

"Ouch!"

"Hi," Willi said with a big smile. My stomach churned with exquisite squiggles, and the inner turmoil sent me fleeing to the restroom.

When I came back, Willi and Steffi had introduced themselves. Steffi looked at me with wide eyes, and with a slight nod of her head she gave me to understand that she approved of Willi.

Willi was sitting straight across from me. My Black-Forest-Cherry-Torte lay submissively before me, but I couldn't eat.

"I know what you want to know," Willi said.

"Tell me everything."

Willi's father worked for the city, he explained. From the department that keeps files on the movement of the populations in and out of Venusbrunn he was able to get the name of the man who had come looking for his aunt. He even had his mailing address.

"Gee, that's great Willi."

"Now what?" Steffi asked.

"We have to write to him."

"What do we tell him?"

"What you know."

"What does she know?" Willie asked, trying not to

49

sound snoopy.

"We can't tell you. Not yet."

"But what if I tell him and then it's not true?" Steffi asked.

"But you said..."

"I know. But, suppose I'm wrong?"

I felt as if I were being doused with ice water. All my excitement and enthusiasm washed down the drain, diluted by worry, frozen by doubt.

"Chicken! Willie, thanks a lot. You've been a real friend. And some day you'll find out just how much you helped us."

"When will that be?"

"I don't know yet."

"Can I see you again?" he asked, and his eyes looked so deep into mine that my stomach started up again.

"I don't know," I spluttered.

"We could meet by the gate some time."

"All right."

"How about every Wednesday at 3:25, or a little earlier, so we have more time to talk."

"We can try. But remember: if you don't see me, it's because there's danger."

"Fair enough."

"Steffi, we have to write to that man," I insisted on the way back to the convent.

"Why do we have to?"

"Because we want to prove that you're not crazy, remember?"

"O.K. But you do it."

"No. You're the one who knows."

"Oh, all right. But what if I'm wrong?"

"You're not wrong," I said while wondering how I could be so sure. Suppose that what I felt was nothing but a wish for adventure. But this thing had gone too far to chicken out now. "We tell him that we think somebody is buried under the stick pile. What's the worst that can happen?"

"That he thinks we're crazy."

"So what else is new."

Steffi laughed. It was a freeing sort of laugh, as though being crazy was fun, not a threat. She straightened up and began walking faster with a shot of new resolve.

Sunday afternoon was letter-writing time, and every head was bent over a piece of paper. It was very time-consuming trying to think of something to write while there was nothing to tell. Steffi wrote to Herr Mueller's nephew that she knew he was looking for his aunt, and that she knew there was a body buried under the great pile of sticks in Herr Mueller's yard.

"Let him put two and two together. That way, I haven't accused anybody of anything," Steffi said when I had finished reading it. A whiff of bad odor reached my nose. I looked up and saw Ellen walking by. Quickly, I hid the letter in my desk. From the expression on her face, though, I could tell that I hadn't been fast enough. "Get away!" I hissed at her.

"Must you always be snooping around?" Steffi said to her.

"If you didn't have something to hide, you wouldn't think I was snooping," Ellen hissed back.

"I hope she doesn't snitch on us," Steffi mumbled as I stashed the letter inside my history book. Lotte would mail it for us. Only letters to parents were allowed to leave the convent uncensored. I should have known, though, that using the boarding school address for a sender would not be a good idea.

Since the weather was too wet for a walk we pulled out our knitting projects, pullover sweaters in the latest fashion stitch with red yarn. The other girls finished one by one and pulled out their needlework. Sister Angela had brought her favorite book, for enlightenment, she claimed, but I figured it was to keep us quiet. Mechtild had brought a new supply of jokes from the butchers in her father's meat market. I could always tell when Mechtild was telling butcher jokes: she would tell them in whispers, then there'd be a moment of silence while the others tried to figure out the sexual connotation, and then would follow embarrassed giggling as one after the other got the drift. Maybe Sister Angela wasn't as dumb as we thought.

"Steffi, you start reading. Everyone will take turns," she said and handed the book to me. The very boring life of St. Theresa of Avila. "Go ahead," she said, seeing that I needed prodding.

I read out loud, not hearing a word I said. Then the other girls in turn read. I still didn't hear very much, until the word clairvoyance made a hit with my ears. I nudged Steffi, "listen to this." It turned out that St. Theresa of Avila was a mystic. She could communicate with spirits, just like Steffi. She almost got burned at the stake for being a witch.

"Dos that mean that St. Theresa was clairvoyant?" I asked Sister Angela that evening. Sister looked pleased that her favorite Saint had made an impression on somebody.

"St. Theresa was a great mystic," she explained with a look of pride as if she knew the Saint herself.

"But, is that the same as being clairvoyant?"

"Not quite. You can be clairvoyant without being a mystic."

"Are there any clairvoyant people around today?" Steffi asked.

"No."

"Why not?"

"These are not the times of saints and mystics," Sister said and turned to scold Roswitha who had failed to camouflage sufficiently the textbook in her lap.

"Why not?" Steffi persisted.

"Why not what?" Sister asked, and it seemed to me

that she was trying to gain time.

"Why are there no clairvoyant people today?"

"We live in different times..." Sister went off to shush Ellen whose laughter was filling the room.

"Boy, would I ever like to tell her a thing or two," Steffi hissed.

"What's it like to be told you don't exist?" I asked, trying to be funny. Steffi didn't answer. When I looked up from my knitting I saw tears in her eyes. "I guess it isn't funny."

"I had a girl friend in fifth grade," she sniffled. "We were best friends. We told each other everything. I thought she would be my friend forever. But one day, I told her that I could see her aura. It was real pretty and bright, and I told her that it meant something real special. But she never talked to me again."

"I had the same thing happen to me, and I'm not even clairvoyant. I had a girl friend in fourth grade. She was rich, but kind of spoiled. Sometimes, I'd go to her house, and sometimes she'd come to mine. But when fifth grade started and we ended up in different classrooms, we never talked to each other again. Isn't that the weirdest thing?"

When I saw Willi the next time, he told me he really liked me, and his eyes wouldn't let go of me. I felt so self-conscious that I didn't know which way to turn. But talk is cheap, I figured, and with a sudden impulse for teasing I pushed my face right up against his with only the gate between us and asked, "what do you like about me?" I gripped the black bars because I couldn't grip his arms.

"It's the way you come right out and say whatever you think. I wish I could be like that."

"Why can't you? Are you too shy?"

"I don't think I'm shy. Maybe more like cautious."

"Why do you have to be cautious?"

"People. You have to be careful what you say.

People like to make fun of you, or put you down if you're different."

"Are you different?" I asked while thinking welcome to the club.

"That's for me to know and for you to find out," he said and laughed mischievously.

"Come a little earlier, next time," I said.

Willi came every week, and every week my stomach did flip-flops that sent me to the toilet long before he ever showed up. Burning down the beaver lodge became less and less important. Going home for Christmas seemed more like punishment than vacation.

When we returned after Epiphany, which is celebrated on January 5, Ellen, on turning down her bed, found a pig's tail between her sheets. A perfectly clean, curly, rosy little pig's tail. But Ellen screamed with revulsion nonetheless. She refused to sleep in her bed and couldn't be persuaded otherwise until Sister Angela offered to change the sheets for her.

Sister could not quiet us that night, for the speculation about who had done the dastardly deed would not stop. "Don't you look at me!" Mechtild yelled at no one in particular. "Just because we have a butcher shop doesn't mean I'd do such a thing."

Ellen gave me a look that made me worry. "I didn't do it either," I said. "I was the last one to come back. Didn't have a chance. Maybe Susie or Gertraud did it to get back at you for sni..." I suddenly remembered that Ellen's guilt had never been proven.

"Figure out who had a motive, then you'll know who did it," Gusti said matter-of-fact.

Finally, when things had quieted, Steffi and I were able to talk. She had gone back to the bookshop. The owner, a woman by the name of Judith, had explained to her everything she wanted to know. With our bodies hanging out our beds, heads together, she whispered, "Humans are actually spirits. The physical body is just a coat we wear till we die. Then, we live in our spirit bodies until we get a new physical body."

"You have got to be kidding!"

"No. I'm dead serious. But there's more: people like me can do things in their spirit body while still in their physical body." I could see Steffi's eyes sparkling in the light of a half moon.

"And you believe that?" I asked in awe at such stupidity.

"And that's why I can talk to my Grandpa, see?"

"Oh, the Church will call you a witch for sure."

"And burn me at the stake, huh? How about you, Stef? I thought you were my friend."

I didn't like the reproach in Steffi's voice. "I am your friend," I hurried to assure her, but oh, so worried and confused. "How can you be so sure? Just because this Judith woman said so? Maybe she's a witch, too." The words had barely escaped my mouth when I realized what an awful thing I had said. I could have kicked myself. Steffi never let on whether she had heard or not; but the excitement was gone from her voice.

"No, not just because she said so. When she explained it to me, it's as if I had known it all the time. Just forgot that I knew it. You know what I mean?"

"Shhhhhh!" Someone hissed loudly.

"Not really," I whispered. "But what do you talk about with a spirit?" I tried hard not to sound snooty.

"Oh all sorts of things. My Grandpa told me that it's quite beautiful where he is, and that he visits with Grandma. He said I shouldn't cry for him. He's very happy."

"Wow! Do you have to talk out loud for him to hear you?"

"Not really. I could just think and he would know.

But it's weird that way, so I talk out loud."

A slipper came flying our way and only barely missed our heads. "Shut up, you two!"

"And what about all those little fairies you can see?"

"They're in some other kind of world, I forgot what it's called. There's a whole lot of different levels. They're on one level, and my Grandpa is on another."

"Did you tell your parents about it?"

Steffi shook her head, then reeled herself in. I had gotten rather chilled and did the same.

With a sour look, Mechtild claimed her slipper next morning.

Between breakfast and first period, Steffi told me of a plan she had dreamed up. She would – on purpose – fail in all the business courses. At the same time, she would work very hard in music, art, calligraphy, history, and language arts. That, she figured, should tell her parents a thing or two.

And that's what she did. She wrote the most beautiful essays, and they were filled with all the little beings of her special world. Sister Hippo smiled when she read them. Then, she complained that Steffi's creativity could be appreciated much more if she hadn't failed her math test so miserably. Steffi shot me a significant look.

By the time Carneval rolled around, waiting for a letter from Herr Mueller's nephew became torture. To relieve the tension at mail time, Steffi and I recited out loud what we were to memorize for our English class. "Columbus sailed the ocean blue in nineteen hundred ninetytwo." We said it in unison and couldn't help giggling. It got us puzzled looks from the other girls. "Jack and Jill went up the hill to fetch a pail of water…" "How much I love my happy home, my father and my mother….." By this time, all eyes were on us, and the frowns and puzzles on their faces made us laugh only louder.

Sister Angela announced that we eighth graders were to move into the Villa that stood between convent vegetable garden and the blacktop of our ball games. One side of the Villa faced the high stonewall that bordered the front of the entire convent grounds, and the other side of the Villa faced the park. The house priest and his housekeeper sister lived on the main floor. The tenth graders had occupied the upstairs rooms.

"Some of the girls behaved very badly, and they cannot be trusted anymore." Sister Angela said it and lowered her eyes. I knew that look. She had it when Steffi asked what venereal disease is; and she had it when Ellen told about rape in the Warsaw Ghetto; and she had it when Mother Superior talked about the girl who got lured to a man's hotel room.

"Then the big girls are moving over here, right?" I asked, and Sister Angela looked visibly uneasy.

"What did they do?" All eyes were on Sister who squirmed like a worm on a fishhook. It was not our concern, she pointed out. "But how can I be sure not to do the same bad thing, if I don't know what it is?" I persisted with a smothered giggle. Sister turned this way and that, the prissy smile missing from her anxious face, her eyelids lowered to avoid meeting our stares. Then she remembered a chore she had to do in the chapel and left.

For once, all of us were talking about the same thing: what fascinatingly awful thing the big girls had done. "Guys, of course," said Roswitha, unimpressed. She had no interest in the opposite sex.

"But Susie and Gertraud talked to boys and they didn't get moved out of the Villa for it."

"Well, this was a lot worse."

"Who? What? Where?" The questions swarmed around like flies on a rotten corps.

"There are ways…" Gusti warbled.

"Well, tell us," we demanded.

Gusti had heard rumors that boys had been seen in the convent garden and under the dorm windows, even inside the dorm! A collective gasp followed her whispered gossip.

"And they think that we eighth graders are soo innocent," Mechtild said and laughed with a glance in my direction. She knows, was written all over Steffi's face as she looked at me with alarm. I simply shrugged. There was nothing I could do about it.

The switch took place the following Saturday. Several piles of feather beddings made their way across the convent grounds. We chose our rooms at random, and when we were all settled in I realized that Steffi not only hadn't picked the bed next to mine, she hadn't even picked my room. "How come?" I asked her.

"Oh… I don't know," she spluttered.

Hmmph.

Instead of Steffi, I had Ellen for a bed neighbor, which, of course, put a crimp into my late night discussions.

Instead of basins and running water, we had bowls and pitchers atop small, wooden nightstands. That meant we had to be careful not to slosh water around or else the furniture got wet and the nuns would have a fit. We had to remember to reserve some clean water in the tooth cup for brushing, or else we'd end up brushing with dirty, soapy water. We couldn't just plop into bed or the priest, downstairs, would complain. I knew that he was hard of hearing, and that made me think he was, therefore, hard of everything else, too. What a mistake that turned out to be!

I was anxious to get to the park to meet Willi. Steffi and I had done chores; the other girls had gone on a long walk up Beuchenberg behind the convent. The day was bright and sunny. Fresh snow had turned the park into a pristine sanctuary. There wasn't a spoiling footprint anywhere. The gate had lost much of its cover of summer growth. The garden was deserted. No one was in sight.

Willi showed up with a broad smile, and I was straining to keep mine from jumping clear off my face. We talked about nothing much in particular, and it seemed to me we behaved like a couple of fishermen who throw out words like bait in hopes of catching something worthwhile. Willi wanted to know, and he always wanted to know, what I couldn't tell him yet. He pretended to have a secret, too, and he would tell it to me when I told him mine.

Suddenly, Willi's face dropped; he jumped back and ducked. I whirled around and saw Sister Elisabeth coming. From her speed I could tell that she was not out for a stroll but had a definite aim: to get me. I tried to act innocent as I walked toward her, hoping to give Willi a chance to get away.

"Who is that by the gate?" she asked.

"Nobody," I lied.

She hurried to the gate and looked out across it. Willi had snug away, but only an idiot wouldn't have noticed the trampled snow on both sides of the gate. Sister looked as though she suspected the devil in person. "Mother Superior will want to talk to you," she said and motioned me to follow her.

We passed the Villa on the way back. I noticed a window curtain closing on the ground floor, and I knew whom to thank for sending me to Superior Court.

To lie or not to lie, that was the question. Paula, one of my older sisters, always said that if you stick to the lie long enough, people will doubt the truth. I planned to test that sibling wisdom.

Sister Elisabeth left me waiting in the reception room. The air was very stale, and the chairs very uncomfortable. I wished Steffi were guilty with me; purgatory would seem much friendlier.

There was a noticeable draft when the door opened

and Mother Superior roared in. "You have deliberately broken the rules once again," she shouted. "You were talking to boys, don't deny it."

"Just one," I said, resigned to tell the truth. It was easier. By setting the record straight, though, I had committed another crime: impudence. I didn't care anymore. Once in hot water, I figured, things couldn't get any worse.

"You know that it is against the rules; you were warned often enough, but you chose to be disobedient. You are not at all like your sister Erna." I could have laughed; that was supposed to make me feel bad? "And to make matters worse, you lied about it. I will notify your parents. In the meantime, you will not be allowed to go to town; and you will not be allowed in the park. You will work in the kitchen every day after dinner for the rest of the month. Now go."

Steffi had seen Sister Elisabeth coming in and me slinking in after her. She had listened and waited near the door. I filled her in while we went to the dining hall together. "I'm so sorry," she said, put her arm around my waist and pressed her face against my arm.

"Oh, I don't care. Pots and pans don't scare me; I'm used to them from home. And my parents aren't going to say much, I know. I talk to the guys in our warehouse all the time. But I can't see Willi for who knows how long. That's a bummer."

The kitchen was huge, and the pots and pans were enormous. The stainless steel sink was as big as a tub, and there were not one but two immense wood cooking stoves with steel tops that required a steel wool rub and a polish. My long braids kept swishing around in the dirt, and my flat feet ached from so much standing. It was a ghastly and lonely chore without Steffi to keep me company. When I was done I had just enough strength left to drop into bed. No more going to town; no more goodies from Café Pole;

no more visits with Willi. I sent word to him through Lotte.

One night, Steffi came slinking into the kitchen. "Well, look what the cat dragged in," I said gleefully. "What are you doing here?"

"Mother Superior found out," a sullen Steffi mumbled.

"What did she find out?"

"About the letter."

"Wow! Tell me about it."

Herr Mueller's nephew had written to Mother Superior. Mother Superior had called Steffi to the "living room" and had ranted and raged about her outlandish accusation, and the embarrassment it had caused them all, and how the man could sue for slander. She had ordered Steffi to write a letter of apology, but Steffi insisted on waiting till she had a chance to talk to her parents. Of course, they had been notified.

"You know what you should do?" I said.

"Scrub the pots," she answered stoically.

"Yeah, I guess you're right." We were quiet for a while, only banging about with the pots.

"You're not scared anymore," I said with sudden insight. Steffi crawled out of the pot she was cleaning. She looked at me, hair hanging in her hot, sweaty face, her apron all rumpled and wet with the straps falling off her narrow shoulders, in her grimy little hand a rusty steel pad. She stood proud and tall, and her face was serene, even happy, as though she just now realized that fear was no longer a threat. Then, she nodded, smiled her impish little grin and went back to scrubbing.

What Steffi had written to Herr Mueller's nephew sent shock waves through the convent. The girls were asking questions, and since the cat was already out of the bag, Steffi said that it was time to open the sealed envelopes. When we felt safe, Helga, Marlies, Ellen, and I, with envelopes in hands, went to Steffi's room.

The girls opened the envelopes by flashlight. First, there was silence while everyone read. Then came a storm of questions. Mechtild and Marlies wanted to know, exactly, how Steffi knew that there were bodies buried under the beaver lodge. Gusti and Roswitha were skeptical. Helga wished that her parents' graves were marked as well as the one in Herr Mueller's yard. Ellen didn't seem very surprised. She thought it was hilarious and wished she could go and dig up the bodies herself.

"Say, Ellen," I whispered to her." How did you know we were going to see Herr Mueller? And you seemed to know some other things too."

"You really want to know?"

"No. I'm just asking because I have nothing better to do."

Ellen laughed. "I can lip read. You didn't know that, did you."

"Wow! Where did you learn that?"

"From my uncle. He can't hear."

"We better get back to our beds now."

I lay awake for a while, trying to figure out if I had anything to fear from Ellen. She probably knew about Willi, and if she had snitched on Susie and Gertraud, she could snitch on me, too. But I hadn't been found out, which meant that Ellen probably hadn't snitched on Susie and Gertraud either. Perhaps I was safe.

Whispering continued in Steffi's room until Sister Fallada, who was in charge in the Villa, went in and demanded to know who had talked. Only Roswitha admitted anything. She might as well have pleaded guilty to praying; Sister dished out no punishment to her. There were no more aphids left, anyway.

Mother Superior summoned our parents by telephone. Steffi's Father couldn't get away from his business, though. "Chicken?" I asked Steffi.

"I think so," she answered with a sigh of relief.

Certainly my Father could not be expected to leave his business, and Mother could not get away either. My baby brother was sick with the measles. But she called to lecture me again on the virtues of obedience.

Wads of crumpled paper went flying every which way when Steffi wrote that letter of apology to Herr Mueller's nephew. Getting frustrated, she sat back and said out loud: "I'm not going to apologize for what I haven't done. But it has to satisfy Mother Superior." She started again, threw it away, started fresh, tossed it, but finally, she handed me the finished version.

"Very clever," I had to admit after reading it. "You only apologize for having caused a problem by talking about the bodies." Steffi looked at me with a confident smile. It made me feel lonely and rejected; I sensed that she would no longer need me.

Then, one day, as we finished dinner and got up to leave, we could see through the window an ambulance parked across the street. Paramedics carried the old man from his house on a stretcher.

"Is he dead?" we asked Sister Angela.

"I don't know anything about it," she answered.

"How can we find out?"

"Never mind Herr Mueller. Shorthand and typing should be your concern," Sister said and looked firmly at Steffi.

Steffi nudged me, "looks like we won't need a shovel after all," she said with a gleam in her eye.

"Let's just hope he doesn't recuperate and live to be a hundred."

"Oh no! Don't say that!"

Lotte brought me a letter from Willi. He wrote that he missed seeing me, and the words he used and the thoughts he expressed were so beautiful that I wondered if it was possible to fall in love with someone's mind. He said that the City had plans to build a new high school on the old man's property. The neighboring gardens had already been bought up, and Herr Mueller had deeded his property to the city some years ago with the understanding that he could remain in his house till he died.

I read Willi's letter in the toilet room after each and every class period. I sniffed it and studied it and carried it around all day, tucked into my bra. By evening, I had memorized it. Then I tore it in teeny-tiny bits and flushed it down the toilet.

Two days later, Sister Angela remarked as we sat together, gossiping and knitting socks, that Herr Mueller from across the street was in the hospital and not expected to live.

"Yesss!" Steffi shouted as she shot out of her seat.

"She's falling apart, I knew she would," Mechtild said with a sneer.

"Oh, let her be," Ellen said. "You just can't stand it that she knows something you don't."

"She knows exactly nothing," Marlies said.

"Sour grapes?" Gusti remarked.

"Girls, that's quite enough," Sister said soothingly. "If Herr Mueller does not return we will have new neighbors."

"Yeah, the City will build a new high school on the old man's property," I blurted out.

"How do you know," Roswitha asked.

"Oh, just a lucky guess," I said, worried sick that I had given away something crucial. Ellen gave me a funny look.

Steffi rescued me with, "I told her. I know all sorts of things, you know. Even the future."

"Oh, sure you do." Marlies sneered at her.

"I predict," Ellen said with comically solemn voice and dignity, "that the stick pile will be removed before the foundation is dug."

"Very funny," Steffi said, and her short laugh sounded forced.

"And I predict," Mechtild added, "that Steffi, with her bad grades and wild imagination, will end up in the loony bin, overwrought and underprivileged."

"Where she will die from nervous hysteria of the solar plexus," added Roswitha dryly. We cracked up laughing.

"You don't have to wait for that to happen. Just take away her stuffed animals and she'll crack right here and now," said a contemptuous Mechtild. I felt like slapping her across the face. Sister said mildly, "now, now girls. That's quite enough of that."

Ash Wednesday had come and gone, and we were in the midst of Lenten season, the six weeks before Easter when good little Catholics do a lot of praying, and fasting, and offering to God anything that is disagreeable. What a clever way to keep us in line!

The old man had died, and bulldozers had begun to level his shack and the gardens that surrounded it. The beaver lodge had been pushed out of the way like so many matches. We were on pins on needles, waiting for ground to be broken.

On the bench under the Linden tree, Steffi and I talked about what Judith had said: that humans have many lives, that we are spirits, that our bodies are just coats that we throw away when they are worn out. Then, why do we have funerals, I wondered. All that hoopla, just to get rid of an old coat? It was all so weird. "What do we need a lot of lives for, anyway?" I asked her.

"To become perfect, Judith said."

"Perfect what?"

"Perfect people, I guess," Steffi said, a little unsure. I must have looked like the proverbial doubting Thomas, because she added with a frown, "you believed me when I

65

told you about the fairies."

"Well, I couldn't help myself. You were so sad and pitiful. And besides, it's fun to think that there are little creatures running about, doing their own little things right under our noses. But more than one life? That's different." She turned her back toward me, miffed. "It's easy for you," I added. "You didn't grow up with a lot of religion. But I did, and this stuff about many lives is just too weird."

"Well, I don't care anymore," Steffi said, got up and walked back to the convent. I felt rejected as I watched her walking away. I sat a while longer, waiting for who knows what. Pretty soon, I started walking. The rhythm of walking usually helped my thinking. The path followed the long side of the park, and soon I came to the spot, which had aroused such awesome feelings of sadness. I stopped, closed my eyes to shut out the world, went deep within to recapture the memory of that sensation, and for just an instant I felt the sadness again. No matter how hard I tried, though, I could not figure out what it meant or why it was.

We were scheduled to go home for Easter vacation on the Wednesday before Easter Sunday. During the previous week, a power shovel had begun to dig up the ground across the street. Steffi and I were watching from the windows every chance we got. The other girls had become infected with our obsession and began watching too. And then, on Thursday, a couple of police cars lines up, and some other trucks and vehicles appeared, and a lot of men moved around the spot where the beaver lodge had been, and they all looked down into a hole in the ground. "That's it!" I shouted. "Now we'll know for sure!"

Our patience was sorely tested. Not until Monday afternoon did Sister Fallada come during study period and motion Steffi to follow her. I nearly died from the squirming in my stomach, waiting, unable to concentrate on anything. Where was Steffi? What were they doing with

66

her? Who wanted her? I felt left out, overlooked, ignored, and it bugged me to no end. After all, I was the one who started all this. I was the one who gave Steffi the courage. Well, maybe I didn't give it to her – more like helped her find it. But I was the one who got her to take action. I should be included. It wasn't fair!

When Steffi finally came back, we couldn't talk right away, but the shine in her eyes told me enough. A little while later, she got up to go to the restroom, and she motioned for me to follow her. She was practically bouncing off the walls when I came in. She could hardly talk, so shaky was her voice with emotion. "Guess what?" she said, and her elfin eyes gleamed, and her face was all lit up with the biggest smile I had ever seen on her.

"They found the body!" I yelled. Steffi nodded. Her body was trembling with suppressed excitement. She grabbed me and I grabbed her, and we hugged and almost squeezed the life out of each other.

"So, tell me."

"They found two skeletons, one adult and one baby. Nobody knows yet who they are. They're investigating. The Police came and wanted to know how I knew about the bodies. They had found out from Herr Mueller's nephew. So I told them. They looked kind of funny, but I was right, so there was nothing they could do but believe me." Steffi sounded utterly triumphant.

"Now your parents will find out."

"That's o.k. The time is right."

Sister Angela's voice nearly snapped that evening as she tried to keep us from getting too noisy. The whole convent knew now that Steffi was right, and that she knew things no one else knew. All sorts of speculations made the rounds. Every story about unusual people that anybody had ever heard was dug up and retold. The skeptics wanted to know exactly how Steffi knew, but she couldn't explain it, and so they remained skeptical.

Tuesday was cleaning day. We took all the desks out of the classrooms and cleaned them. Then we scrubbed the wooden floors with water and soap, which removed the old wax and some of the color. When the wood had dried we applied stain to restore the color. When the stain had dried we applied a layer of thick, heavy wax, by hand, on our knees. When the wax had been absorbed we polished the floor with the help of a Blocker, a thick, rectangular thing that was very heavy and was studded with very short, hard, dense bristles. Pushing it back and forth by a long, stiff handle required some strength.

The work took all day. When we dropped into bed late that night Sister Angela had no trouble keeping us quiet. We were out like lights.

Wednesday was packing day. During the morning, Sister Fallada came to take Steffi out of class again. Sister wore the kind of smile that nuns put on when parents come for a visit, all friendly and caring and fake. "Now what?" Steffi whispered as she looked at me, puzzled.

Steffi never returned to class. I felt pretty rejected. Going to lunch without her, nobody to talk to. We were lined up and waiting to enter the dining hall when she came running toward me, grabbed my hand and pulled me along. "What's going on?" I asked.

"You'll see," she said, and laughed as she dragged me to the reception room where Mother Superior, Sister Fallada, and her parents were waiting.

It had to be a good sign; Steffi was too happy for it to be otherwise. She introduced me to her parents who were very friendly and polite. They were planning to have dinner in town and Steffi had asked that I be invited.

While we went to get our coats, Steffi told me that her parents had been notified of everything. "And I mean, everything," she said with emphasis. "About my grades, and about the trouble we got into, and about the buried bodies, and the letter, and everything…"

"What did they say?"

Her face took on a pensive look. "Stef," she said.

"What?"

"I'm not coming back after Easter."

"Whaaat?"

"My parents decided to put me in a pedagogical school where I can study music, too."

"You have got to be kidding!"

"They're convinced now that I'm no good in business. My trick worked."

"But Steffi....!"

"In my state, the new school year starts after Easter; it's perfect timing, see?"

"But Steffi....!"

"I know. I'm going to miss you too," she said and hugged me, and I hugged her, and water came rushing into my eyes.

"Come on, you two," said Sister Fallada, her fake smile intact. "Don't keep your parents waiting."

Steffi's parents' Mercedes was parked at the curb. We climbed in, and nobody said much on the way to Hotel Bavaria. The tables were set with white linens and real silver ware, and the waiters were dressed in black suits. I would have felt just grand any other time, but now I was too upset about losing Steffi.

Her Father said I could order anything I wanted. I ordered my favorite, Sauerbraten, red cabbage, and potato dumplings with lots of gravy.

"Stephanie will attend a teacher training school," her father explained. "She can take voice lessons there while she studies to become a teacher."

"If I don't make it as a singer, I can always teach singing, see?" Steffi said with much enthusiasm. I couldn't help but be happy for her.

"Can I come to visit?" I asked

" Of course. Steffi told us that you live in Hanfurt.

That's not very far from Wiesenthal. You might not even have to change trains," her Father said.

"And you can come and visit me," I said politely, though I figured it would be much more fun for me to visit Steffi. She had neither nasty big sisters nor pesky little brothers.

Steffi's Mother said, "we were so relieved when we learned that Steffi had a good friend here. When she came home for Christmas we noticed a good change in her. Thanks to you, we now know that Steffi is not – well, you know. We have a lot to learn yet about Steffi and her ways.

When we returned to the convent, I was allowed to help Steffi pack. We climbed the stairs to the attic when she mentioned Willi. "Don't worry about him, I said. "I've got it all figured out. I'm going to ask him to come to the Public Library on Saturdays. Good plan, huh?"

Steffi nodded silently.

"But oh, how I'm going to miss you! You are so much fun with your fairies, and your Grandpa, and dead bodies." Steffi grinned self-consciously.

I took her things from her closet and she put them in the suitcase. Then she moved them around, stuffed socks into the gaps around the edges, folded and refolded her Sunday dress three times before she was satisfied. Then she realized that she had forgotten to put in her shoes first, so we put them in the bottom of her laundry bag. She picked up her suitcase, then, and I grabbed her laundry bag, and we headed for the stairs.

"Wait a minute, Steffi," I said and motioned her to sit with me on a large trunk. "I've been doing a lot of thinking. I don't think that it's fair for you to expect me to believe everything you tell me. I can only believe what seems right to me, not just because somebody else says so, don't you think?"

Steffi nodded quietly.

"You don't believe some things either, like babies

going to limbo if they die before they're baptized, right?"

"I sure don't."

"And you won't believe it just because the Church says so, right?" I knew that it was her pet peeve.

"Yeah, that's just too much. How can you keep perfectly innocent little babies out of heaven just because some priest hadn't dribbled any water on them yet!"

"That's how I feel about living more than one life. I do believe some of the things you told me. But this is just a bit much for me."

"You're absolutely right. And you know what? You don't have to. It's not important to our friendship, right?"

"Right. Besides, maybe some day I'll change my mind. Maybe I'll find out for myself."

"You know what my Grandpa said? That we must always change our mind."

"He wants us to be wishy-washy?"

"No. Not that. See, he meant that whenever we get more information about something, then we'll understand it better."

"I get it. And when you understand it better, you might change your opinion about it."

"Yeah, that's what he meant. So, someday, when you learn more about the unseen world you'll change your mind. And right now, it's enough for me to know that you don't think I'm crazy," she said with her impish smile.

"I never thought you were crazy."

"Thanks, Stef, I know."

Her parents stowed away the suitcase in the trunk of the Mercedes while Steffi said good-bye to the nuns and the other girls. Then I walked her to the car. "Remember to write," I whispered.

"Through Lotte," she whispered back with a sweet-sour smile of joy and apprehension. Her Father started the car, turned it around, and off they went, I waved till they had disappeared around the bend.

The next twenty-four hours were murder. My stomach had tied itself in knots from losing Steffi, and then it got all squirmy from thinking about Willi, and I didn't know if I was coming or going. Through Lotte I had let him know when I would be at the station. I was planning to miss my train and take a later one. It would give us a chance to spend some time together in the station's waiting room without worry about being seen and found out.

I got to the station with my hands sore and my arms nearly numb from carrying my heavy suitcase which, I had figured, would make me look important – long journey, great distance, that sort of thing. I went to the third class dining room and ordered some apple juice. I had pinned my braids across the top of my head again. My nose, which just yesterday had tried hard to produce a large pimple, had decided otherwise. I felt good.

Willi showed up, huffing and puffing from running all the way from his high school. He attended the Upper Secunda, the Latin name for the eleventh grade, he explained to me. His school taught Latin, and every grade level had a Latin name. He had two more years to go, and then he would study philosophy at the University.

He sat down opposite me and just stared at me with a blissful smile. The effect on my stomach was almost unbearable. "It's been a long time," he said.

"I know," was all I could muster with an unsteady voice. Then I remembered that I owed him an explanation. "I can tell you now," I said.

"Tell me what?"

"You know; our secret about Herr Mueller."

"Oh yes, tell me about him. And then I have something to tell you, too."

"I thought you made that up."

"No, I didn't," he answered, laid his arms on the table in front of him and said, "go ahead."

"First, tell me the latest about Herr Mueller."

Willi knew that an investigation was going on, and that there was talk that Herr Mueller had murdered his wife and perhaps even a baby. Possibly his own. Willi's Grandmother remembered that, a long time ago, she had thought that Mrs. Mueller was pregnant. But when a baby never materialized she figured it had been just fat.

"My friend Steffi knew about the bodies," I told Willi.

"Everybody knows about them."

"No. I mean, she knew about them long before they were dug up. She actually told Herr Mueller's nephew about them. That's why we wanted his address."

"How did she know?" Willi asked and straightened up. He seemed to be listening with his whole body.

"She's clairvoyant," I replied, proud to have mastered that world. I figured he was going to have all sorts of questions and doubts and arguments about what I had said. Instead, Willi said nothing. He leaned back and smiled so sweetly that I would have followed him to the ends of the earth that very minute.

"Did you believe Steffi?"

"Yes."

"How come?"

"Oh, I don't know. Maybe I felt sorry for her."

"Do you always believe people just because you feel sorry for them?"

I had to think about that for a moment. "No, I guess not."

"Then why did you believe what Steffi told you?" Willi asked, leaning forward and watching me intently.

He was getting a little too deep for me. "I don't really know," I confessed. "I don't know why I believe that there are fairies and gnomes and elves, either. I just like to think that they exist. You know, makes life more interesting. She used to tell me the funniest stories about them."

"Did you ever think that whatever our minds can come up with must already exist?" Willi said, and now he had lost me completely. I felt like a first-grader having a conversation with the Pope. He noticed the empty look on my face and leaned back, saying: "I can tell you stories about fairies and gnomes and elves, too."

"Oh, you could never tell them as well as Steffi. You'd have to see them first."

"Over there, on that table," he said and pointed to a piece of leftover coffee cake. "A little gnome is roping himself up to the chair seat, like a mountaineer. He's got the cutest little grappling hook and he's swinging it around and around - now it's hooked onto the tabletop. He's pulling himself up like a real pro, and all that time, a tiny shadow fairy is clapping her hands and cheering him on. Now he's on top, running over to that plate. He's stuffing the cake into his little backpack; now he's roping himself down again... Over there, by the coat stand, is his tiny house. His little wife is watching him. She's calling to him to be careful. Now he's down, rewrapping his ropes... stowing his grappling hook. His little wife has gone back into the house and he's following her. And the shadow fairy is dancing on the table...."

Then, with a twinkle in his eyes, looking straight at me, he said, "and your aura is bright and beautiful."

I had been home for summer vacation for just two weeks when I felt like running back to Venusbrunn. Every time I tried to capture a bit of attention, which took speed and excellent timing with seven siblings around, Erna butted in. When the boys from Father's business flirted with me she called me names. When Mother was late with an errand, Erna pointed to me and I had to do the running. When Father wanted more beer late at night Erna managed to disappear, and I was sent to the cellar. A musty, dingy, eerie dungeon it was, with only one miserly light bulb that threw more shadows than it illuminated. And when Erna didn't feel like waxing the kitchen floor Mother told me to do it. It seemed logical to her since my hands were dirty already from washing and waxing the stairway.

And it got worse. Willi wrote a letter to me, and Erna was in charge of the mailbox key. One day, Paula, who was only nineteen but getting married a few days later, lay sick on the sofa. Erna was twenty but didn't even have a steady boyfriend. I came into the living room and found Erna reading something to Paula. When she noticed me, she quickly hid it behind her back, and that's what tipped me off. I demanded my letter.

"I haven't read it yet," Erna replied with a triumphant snicker. I demanded my letter again.

"And Mother hasn't read it yet."

My hand shot out and slapped her so hard that her glasses went flying. Paula grinned gleefully while Erna went searching for her glasses. The letter fell to the floor and I picked it up and ran from the room. Of course Erna ran crying to Mother, and of course Mother yelled and blamed me for the broken glasses.

I hated Erna's guts. Every time she got into the car I wished she'd have an accident and never come back. But wishful thinking wouldn't get me anywhere. It would have been nice to have an accomplice with whom to plot and scheme and dream up dastardly deeds. But Paula was getting married and didn't care anymore. Seventeen-year-old Walter learned the business out of town. He was the oldest son and heir apparent. That gave him an aura of importance that Erna didn't dare mess with. Hans was only twelve and oblivious to Erna's bad habits. He lived in his own little world, somewhere between illusion and reality. Elfriede was eight and loved Erna. Heaven only knows why. Matthias and Markus were too little to be useful for anything.

So there I was, fifteen, alone in a house full of eight kids, and no one for company. I missed Willie, missed the peace and order of the convent, Sister Angela's intense smiles and her earnest disappointment when I had misbehaved. I missed the old trees in the convent park and the mysterious sensations that I had felt at the old mill.

At home, my feelings got squashed by indifference. Mother had nothing but work and responsibilities for me. Father was never present even if his body was; when he did agree to play a board game with us it was only to finish it and win. The little kids wouldn't listen to me and got me in trouble. Erna poisoned the atmosphere with her hatefulness. Paula escaped to her fiancé every chance she got.

"Could I invite Steffie to visit me?" I asked Mother. "That's out of the question," she called back over her shoulder as she hurried down the stairs because Father was waiting with the car to take her to the garden.

It was Saturday afternoon. Business was closed and life was quiet in preparation for Sunday. Mother had given me four things to do, and I had just completed the third one. I stopped at the fourth-floor stairway window, propped my arms on the sill and tried to recall the fourth one. The window looked out over a narrow, dingy courtyard that was hemmed in by our four-story warehouse on two sides and our four-story house on the other two. I could escape the ugliness by looking at the blue sky and watch the movement of the clouds. The song of a Thrush embellished the afternoon stillness and made me think of Willi with his gorgeous blue eyes and sweet smile.

When I noticed the laundry fluttering on the lines that were strung across the flat warehouse roof I remembered the fourth chore: take down the laundry. At that very moment, Mother saw me from our kitchen window. Seeing me there with my arms propped comfortably on the windowsill, she shocked me out of my sweet meditation with her angry voice, which accused me of being lazy. While I took down the laundry Mother's harsh and unfair condemnation began to get under my skin. By the time I got back to my room that I shared with Hildegard tears were running down my face. I stood at the window, staring out at nothing, floundering in great misery that shook my body. I could not stop crying.

When I finally collected myself, I felt something shutting down inside me. A resolve took hold of me as if something or someone else had taken command of me. I changed into my Sunday clothes, put on hose and shoes, grabbed my little bag which held my return railroad ticket, and left the apartment unseen and unheard. I headed straight for the railroad station and took the next train to Venusbrunn.

It was getting dark as I walked to the convent, tears steadily running down my face. Sister Angela opened the convent doors, dumbfounded to see me in the middle of the summer. "Stephanie! How did you get here? Why are you here? Do your parents know?" Her words expressed such deep affection and caring that it intensified what I could not put into words then, a loneliness that was beyond description. She took me to the living room, and then went to fetch Mother Superior.

Mother Superior was surprisingly gentle. She gave me time to calm down and then questioned me about what had happened. But I didn't know what had happened.

Nothing had happened, nothing out of the ordinary, anyway. "I'm glad you came here instead of going somewhere else," she finally said. Then she went to call my parents to let them know that I was safe.

Sister fixed me something to eat in the kitchen, then she unlocked the washroom and the dorm room, and I got ready for bed. She wished me a good night, but it was long in coming. I lay with my eyes open and savored the peace and order and harmony that were so intense in this quiet isolation. And the misery took hold of me again.

Father and Mother came early next morning. I could see them from the window as they climbed out of the car. While they waited for the door to open I could see Father talking to Mother. Mother Superior would receive them first, I knew.

They talked for a long time. Finally, Sister came to get me. I felt like crawling into a hole to never come out again. What would I say? How would I explain? I didn't really understand why I had run away. There was just this deep misery for which I had no words.

I walked into the living room where I had spent many anxious moments waiting for Mother Superior to storm in. The window stood open, and a fresh breeze filled the usually stuffy room with its hard, stiff, straight furniture of yesteryear. Father, Mother, and Mother Superior sat on chairs around the table. Sister Angela had me sit on the fourth one, and then she left the room. I stared at the pattern of the lace tablecloth and tried to figure out the knitting stitches that had been used to make it, while Mother Superior talked, and Father talked. When he could not get much more than "I don't know" out of me he gave up. Mother said nothing, which was unusual, and when I ventured a glance I saw her angry eyes on me.

"Perhaps a visit with your girl friend would be good for you," Mother Superior suggested, and it was the first comment that made contact with my mind.

"Would you like that?" Father asked, while Mother clamped her mouth shut.

"Yeah, that would be great!" I said, overjoyed. I began to sense that, right now, I was holding a position of some power. "Could she come and visit for a while? I promise I'll still do my chores. Steffie could even help me. I'm sure she won't mind." I looked to Father who nodded thoughtfully. He glanced at Mother whose eyes had given up their piercing activity. Steffie could come and visit for a couple of weeks in early August, Mother agreed.

Paula was married by then, so Steffie and I were allowed to use hers and Erna's room. Erna was livid about it. "You just better leave my things alone," she warned with an evil eye while she packed up a two-week supply of her stuff. I had visions of putting mousetraps in her underwear drawer.

On a Friday late afternoon I picked up Steffie at the railroad station and brought her to our apartment on the third floor. I introduced her to whoever happened to be at home, and then we went to our room downstairs.

"Where are we going?" Steffie asked.

"You'll see," I said as I led the way to Erna's room on the second floor. When Father had the second floor apartment converted into offices, one room was made into a bedroom/living room for my two elder sisters. It had a modern sofa that doubled as a bed, and a modern tile floor, and modern wallpaper with graphic design, and it even had a washbasin near the door. The toilet was straight across the hall. It had to be shared with the office staff. Compared to a family of two adults and eight children sharing one toilet, Erna's room had great privacy.

Steffie was still smaller than I and a bit on the delicate side, but she had gained some weight since she left the boarding school at Easter time. She held her head high now and wore her dark hair shoulder-length, the ends curled under. Her eyes were just as big and black as I remembered them. She seemed older now, or more mature. She was definitely much happier then when I first laid eyes on her scrawny, skittish little self back in Venusbrunn.

We hugged and giggled and talked as loud as we wanted in our own private four walls. Not that it was a big deal to her. Steffie always had privacy because she was an only child.

"Are you still planning to be a singer?" I asked, slightly jealous of so much opportunity.

"Sure am," she said. "How about you?"

"Business. That's it. My parents don't know anything else. Mother says it won't hurt to know about it."

"How are things with Willi?"

"Oh! Talking about Willi! You know what my sister Erna did?" I spilled it all, every contemptible bit of it. Steffie was even more outraged than I; she was not used to abominable acts of a sibling kind.

"What are you going to do about it?" she asked.

"Get even—as soon as I can think of something deliciously nasty. And you're gonna help me, right?"

"That's what friends are for." We shook hands on it.

"Come on, I'll show you around. I bet you've never seen a home that's strung out over as many floors as ours."

We went out to the hallway, nosed around the offices, tried out the machines and checked the view from every window. The archive was the biggest room, an addition to the house, rising above a narrow movie theater. The archive lay at the end of the hallway, ahead of our bedroom and the toilet. Its back window looked out across an empty space between our house and the warehouse. The warehouse wall, which rose three more stories, had just one tiny window that caught Steffie's eye. "What's that?"

"Watch," I said. Then I called, "Herr Fingerle! Are you there?"

In a moment, his head popped through the window, all handsome, with lots of coal-black hair and a 5 o'clock shadow that defined supreme masculinity for me. "What's up?" he called back with an easy smile. "Who's your friend?"

"That's Steffie, my friend from Venusbrunn. She's here for a visit."

"That spells double trouble." Then, directed at Steffie, he added, "I've raised her, you know. And I've helped raise her sisters and brothers, too, all eight of them. I was working here before her mother ever married into the family."

Steffie looked from Herr Fingerle to me and back to him with obvious confusion. "What are you doing there?" she asked.

"This is a projection room. I run the movies. Come on over and check it out some time." With a twinkle in his eyes he vanished from the window.

"Wow! What a weird place," Steffie said.

"That's nothing. Wait till you see the rest."

Next to the toilet room—and toilet was all it contained—a door led to the former kitchen. The former kitchen window was replaced by a door, and through it, across a little iron bridge that connected our house to the warehouse, we made it to a spiral staircase. It connected the movie theater on the main floor with the projection room on the second floor, a warehouse entry on the third floor, and the theater's office on the fourth floor.

Steffie tip-toed across as if she expected it to collapse. Then we scrambled over the stairway, opened the door to the projection room, and there was Herr Fingerle, working his monstrous projection machines, which droned with the muffled sounds of movie dialogue. In the corner, on a small table, invisible hands rewound the weekly newsreel.

"Come on in," he said in his hearty way. I stepped inside the chamber of puzzles and Steffie followed, a little nervous. She soon relaxed though when Herr Fingerle

81

explained that mysterious stuff to her, like he had done plenty of times to us kids. He was the one who had taught us the difference between character and actor. He had also unraveled for us the mystery of why Tom Mix, the original Hollywood Cowboy, could suffer a deadly accident at the end of one movie yet be very much alive in the sequel.

Steffie wanted to see more. I took her down the stairs to the door that led to the back of the theater lobby. Peeking through the door I could see that the curtains were drawn, which meant that a movie was in progress. Frumpy Fraeulein Hartung, the usher, sat against the opposite wall under a dim light and darned socks, which took up her entire attention. I put my finger to my lips and we tip-toed to the left, through the lobby, out into the street.

"Wow! What a great escape route," Steffie said in awe. I wished I had thought of it first.

We had a lot of catching-up to do, and it was late before we got to bed that night. I was just dozing off when, suddenly, Steffie sat up with a start and jerked me awake. "What's the matter?" I asked.

"Oh, I just had one of those awful visions."

"What did you see?"

"Somebody getting run over by a car."

I turned on the lamp on the bedside table. Steffie was moaning, her hands covered her face. "Tell me," I coaxed her gently.

"There was a crowd of people, a procession of some sort, with singing and praying. Then a car comes, goes out of control, and then it hits a girl, or woman, and knocks her down."

"Is she dead?"

"I don't know. I didn't see any more."

"Do you have these visions a lot?" I asked, rubbing her back the way Mother did for my little brothers whenever they were upset.

"Just sometimes. But they're awful. I never know the people I see, so I can't help them." We lay down again. "Judith said that I shouldn't feel bad that I can't help."

"Easier said than done, huh?"

"Right. I asked Judith why I see these things. You remember Judith, don't you? The woman from the book store?"

"The one who knew what you wanted before you ever told her? I remember."

"Well, Judith says that I'm able to tune into the future, and the past, kind of like tuning into radio waves. Problem is, I don't have any real control over it yet. So anything can pop into my head."

"Are you all right now?"

"Yeah, I guess so. Just have to try and forget that face I saw."

Mother had plenty for us to do on Saturday. I had promised her that I wouldn't skip out on chores but have Steffie help me. Steffie didn't mind. We shopped for groceries, carried the big sheet cake to the bakery because it didn't fit our oven, hung up the laundry on the flat roof of the warehouse, fetched wood and coal from the warehouse cellar for heating the bathroom water heater, and we bathed the little kids. Steffie liked that a lot, and when I got tired of leaning over a high tub in a steaming hot bathroom, trying to hang on to a couple of squirming brats, she took over. The kids had more respect for a stranger and held real still for her.

That evening, we were leaning on the broad windowsill of our room and watched people strolling by. It was a clear, warm evening, and sound carried far. My eyes followed the movement down below, up the street, up the street, up the street like wave after wave flowing toward a lakeshore. The movement became hypnotic while the sounds faded.

83

Steffie poked me in the ribs. "What do you do for fun on a Saturday night?"

"I guess we could cool off these poor, sweating souls down there with a bucket of water," I suggested with a giggle. "We might even add a few thumb tacks."

"No, really," she said and laughed. "What do you do on Saturday night?"

"Oh, I have great fun on Saturday nights: I fix supper for the kids and put them to bed, and then I stand guard to make sure they stay put. Unless, of course, Mother goes to the garden, which she does almost every day during the summer. Then we pick fruit and vegetables, buckets full, and bring it all home, then wash it, and pit it, and peel it, and chop it, and grind it, and can it..."

"Enough already," Steffie whined. "But what are we, I mean, me and you, gonna do tonight?"

"How about a walk?"

"How about a movie?"

"How about both? I'll ask Mother."

Mother was a big woman and she had been on her flat feet all day. She said "no." Actually, Mother said, highly incredulous as if I had asked to go to Sidney, Australia, "it's out of the question." Darn it! I should have taken Steffie along. Mother wouldn't have dared to refuse her. She would have put on her phony smile, and cocked her head sideways, and used her sing-songy voice to say "but of course." Steffie would have been charmed out of her wits like everybody else who wasn't family.

I figured it wasn't very considerate toward a guest to bore her to death; and I figured that Mother would have been much more agreeable if she hadn't been so tired; and I figured that it was only right that I should remedy the situation.

"We can see the movie downstairs. The next one starts at 9:00 o'clock. And it won't cost us a thing, " I said to Steffie .

"How come?"

"Because it's our house."

We waited till eight-thirty and then went upstairs to watch the single available television program till almost nine. Then, we yawned really bored, pretended we didn't like the program, said goodnight to my parents and went to our room again.

"Now comes the fun part," I declared and headed for the former kitchen. The door to the escape route was locked. "Darn it!"

"How about the downstairs door? Is it locked?"

"Always at this time of night. And I don't have a key for it."

"Well, then how about that little window in the projection room?" Steffie suggested it with a crafty smile. What a change from her scared little self of Venusbrunn days!

We went to the archive room and climbed out through its broad window. So far, so good. Climbing in through the tiny projection room window, however, proved to be a little harder. Our super full skirts and layers of stiff petticoats wanted to fluff up over our heads instead of staying down over our knees. Meanwhile, I was trying to figure out how to persuade Herr Fingerle to ignore us.

He was working on his machines and looked up just long enough to give us a big smile of recognition, as if there was nothing unusual about people crawling in through his window and walking out through his door. "Just passing through," I mumbled on my way out with Steffie right behind me.

I stopped and signaled Steffie to be very quiet. I had to make sure Mother wasn't looking down from the kitchen or bathroom window. Satisfied, we went down quietly through the side door and into the theater. We found a couple of places in the expensive back rows, and I breathed a sigh of relief. The weekly news was running.

"What about Herr Fingerle?" Steffie whispered to me. "Is he gonna give us away?"

"You know something," I whispered back with a sudden flash of insight. "He didn't seem at all surprised when we came through there."

"Your sisters!" Steffie whispered, and across her face and my face spread great big grins because we had just discovered a naughty secret. "But why do they have to sneak around that way? Don't they have keys?"

"We're not allowed to have keys. Not for the apartment door and not for the downstairs door. If we come home from somewhere and the downstairs door is locked we have to ring the bell, and then my mother wraps the big bundle of keys in a towel and throws it down from a window."

"You have got to be kidding," said Steffie and giggled. But it wasn't funny to me. Standing there on the sidewalk of Hanfurt's favorite promenade, with my face up in the air and people walking by as an unraveling pile of something comes shooting down like a torpedo, causing me to jump aside to avoid getting hit! What if a fine guy came walking by and saw this ridiculous maneuver.

The movie was a Western, like almost every movie that ever came to the Roxy since the end of the war. I loved Westerns. Germany was small and very crowded and full of bomb craters and rubble heaps. Life was one great, big hurry because everything was in short supply including space. But in the darkness of the theater I could escape, at least for a little while, to the wide open spaces of the American West. While other girls dreamed of knights in shining armor, I dreamed of racing across the endless prairie on the back of a black stallion.

It was almost eleven o'clock when the movie was over. "Come on," I said to Steffie. "Now you'll see another escape route." I led her out through Roxy's exit, which led through the loading yard and through a huge, black, solid metal gate out into the side street. We went around to the front of the house and back to Roxy's entry. Steffie was utterly confused.

In the light of street lanterns and the theater marquee, the coming and going motorcycle crowd revved up their machines to a hellish noise. Steffie and I moved into the darkness of the driveway between our house and the neighbor's house, hoping to get a glimpse of the forbidden nightlife.

We had barely made it into the darkness when a couple walked by, their arms around each other so weirdly that I wondered how they were able to move forward without tripping each other up. When I looked from their tangled arms to their faces, my heart nearly stopped. It was Erna with a guy. I poked Steffie in the side and said, "come on, we've got to see this. That's my sister Erna who just walked by. I'm gonna spy on her."

It was easy to keep an eye on Erna and her guy. A row of trees on the left and storefront nooks and crannies on the right provided plenty of cover. They walked up toward the railroad station, then down the other side of the street where two more movie theaters had attracted the motorcycle set to the late show. Wannabe-mother and her guy continued on till they hit University Square, then turned around and came back up to the Roxy. Steffie and I cut across the street to get ahead of them. Then we watched them from the darkness of the driveway.

Soon, I realized that Erna and her guy were steering toward our hiding place. I grabbed Steffie by the arm and pulled her further back where we hid behind the single wild grape vine that had grown to cover most of the four-story wall of the warehouse. We held our breaths.

"Tomorrow? Same time?" I heard Erna saying. She was standing against the wall and had her arms and hands around the guy's waist. I could see her silhouette against the light of the street lantern. She had her hair tied in a silly little knot low on the back of her head, the way mother wore it. And there was no one less stylish than Mother.

"Erna," he said.

"What?" I could hear alarm in her voice.

"I can't see you anymore," the guy said. There was a long pause during which Erna took her hands off him.

"Why not?" she asked, and her voice was shaky now. For a moment, I felt sorry for her.

"I had a girl friend for a long time. On the night that I met you at the dance we had broken up. But now, we made up." The guy sounded fairly sincere.

"So?" Erna's voice was shakier still.

"We've been going steady for a long time. Her parents and my parents expect us to get married. I'm sorry.

Erna cried, of course. Erna always cried. She's built too close to the water, Mother always said. The guy kept talking, trying to get her to stop crying, as if Erna didn't have a good reason for being upset. I really didn't want to hear any more, but we had to stay put till they left.

When we came back through the projection room, I asked Herr Fingerle just how often my sisters had used this fabulous escape route. "A few times," he said and winked at me. "It's none of my business."

Once we got back to our room I realized that Steffie hadn't said a word since we first started trailing Erna. "What's up?" I asked. Steffie looked depressed.

"I know the person from my vision," she said.

"Who is it?"

"It's your sister Erna."

"Yesss!" I yelled. "It's perfect."

"What's perfect?"

"Your vision. You think it was Erna, right?" Steffie nodded. "Well, my problems are over. She gets hit by a car, and I'm rid of her."

"Stef! You can't mean that."

"You wouldn't say that if you had to live with her. And besides, you said you'd help me," I nearly shouted. I feared that she would talk me out of a perfect opportunity.

"Well yes, I know. But Stef, we can't just let her die…"

"Why? You said yourself that Judith said your visions are accidental, and that they have no purpose."

"But this is different."

"Why? Because it's my sister?"

"No. Because I can do something about it. That's why. So I have to."

I came down from my giddy height and flopped on the sofa. "I guess so," I mumbled, disappointed. It was most annoying that Steffie should play guardian angel to my favorite enemy.

"Do you always obey Judith?" I asked. There must have been a sneer in my question because Steffie looked sad when she answered, "no, only when it makes sense to me."

It was past midnight when we got into bed. "So what are we going to do now?" I asked.

"We can't stop an accident from happening, but we can stop your sister from being there," Steffie said. "There were a lot of people around… a parade of some sort… a religious one because I could see some altar boys. Is something like that coming up?"

"I don't know. Corpus Christy is over, and St. Bonifatius, too. We did the fire pilgrimage and the plague pilgrimage. I hate those things. Every year my mother makes us go along just because our stupid ancestors made a promise. Actually, it was more like a bribe. They promised a pilgrimage to the church on the hill if God would stop the plague. It must have worked because then they promised another pilgrimage if he would stop the fire."

"For just a fire?"

"Well, I can understand that. Houses were made of wood then, and they were built real close together. A fire could wipe out a whole town. But anyhow, I can't think of any other. But Mother would know. She never forgets anything the priest announces from the pulpit."

"Ask her tomorrow, okay?" I promised.

But I was in no hurry. Mother made it easy for me. In the morning, we had our usual Sunday chaos, trying to get two adults and too many children ready for Church at the same time in the presence of one toilet and a single clock that didn't keep good time; add to that Father's anger over being late for church, again, and losing out on a good seat, again.

"Ask her," Steffie whispered to me during dinner, but the little kids with their spoons and forks were scraping noises across their enameled dishes while Father was trying to hear the news over a lot of static on the radio in the next room. Mother kept shushing everybody.

"Ask her," Steffie said when we had done the dishes. She jabbed me in the ribs for good measure. But Mother had put me in charge of keeping the other kids out of the living room where she was resting on the couch with Markus in her clutches, trying to force him into a nap while he kept trying to escape.

We took the kids to the park, and on the way we met Erna who was coming back from the post office where she had gotten the mail for Father. I decided to have some fun with her.

"What are you going to do this afternoon?" I asked her.

"It's none of your business," she replied, her lips pulled taught across her teeth.

"Do you have a date with your boyfriend again?"

Erna tripped over the curb and nearly fell down. "What boyfriend?" she said after she caught herself.

"Oh, yeah. I almost forgot. You got dumped again."

Erna raised her long, hard finger, and said, almost choking with rage, "you just better shut up if you know what's good for you, you stupid brat." Then she turned quickly, but not before I saw tears in her eyes.

"Just for that, I'm going to snoop through her things," I said, and after we had herded the kids around the park for a while we took them back home. Then we headed straight for our room.

"She looked so scared," Steffie said, deep in thought as we started to pull out Erna's stuff and pile it on a big heap. Then we looked each item over before putting it back. There was a beautiful silk scarf I had never seen before, and a brand new expensive looking angora sweater. I pulled out her shoes and began to try each pair. When I put on her ski boots, I nearly broke my toe because something hard was stuck inside it. I reached in and pulled out a small box that had the name of a local jeweler printed on it. I opened it and found a gold necklace and two gold rings, one with a blue stone, the other with a purple stone.

"Wow!" said Steffie. "I wonder why she hides it."

"Maybe they are presents from that run-away boyfriend of hers," I said while I tried on the ring. It was too big.

"But why would she hide them?"

"Oh, you don't know my parents. She was probably trying to keep him a secret."

"But why?" Steffie wondered.

"Maybe he's from the wrong family, or maybe he has the wrong profession, or not the right hair color, who knows."

Now that I thought about it, I wondered how Paula had managed to be married at only nineteen when my parents hardly allow us to go on dates. Her new husband was quite a few years older than she, but he had a business of his own. That must have clinched the deal. Erna's has-been boyfriend was probably not a business man. Butcher? Baker? Candlestick maker? Knaves, all three.

"Maybe she was worried that my parents would find out about him. Not that it matters anymore."

"I don't think so. I think it's more than worry. Every emotion shows up as a color in the aura, you know. And her colors are fear and depression."

"She could also be a thief," I said.

"Why? How?"

"She could have bought that jewelry with stolen money."

"Oh oh!"

"Erna works in the store, you know. She handles the cash register. It wouldn't be too hard to do." I put the little box with jewelry back into the ski boot.

Steffie looked at me with sad eyes. She didn't like strife, and she didn't like sadness. And now I wished that I had never snooped around in Erna's things.

Mother said there would be a pilgrimage to the church on Maria Ehrenberg. We would celebrate there the feast of the Assumption of the Blessed Virgin Mary. It was scheduled for the following Sunday.

"Are we all going?"

"Yes, we are all going," Mother said.

"How are we going to manage with just one car?"

"Never mind," Mother said, and I decided to shut up and leave before she thought of something for me to do.

"We have to keep your sister Erna from going," Steffie said while she paced back and forth like a super sleuth. "It should be fairly simple: since you can't all fit into your little VW, somebody has to stay behind. It'll probably be Erna with the little kids, don't you think?"

"You don't know my mother. Everybody will go."

"In one little VW?"

"You should see what we manage. The little kids can be stuffed into the space behind the back seat, three will fit on the back seat with two on their laps, and Mother can have one on her lap in the front. But Erna will probably be driving one of the cars from the business."

"Darn it."

"Unless Paula and her husband are going, too. Then some of us could ride with them, and Erna wouldn't have to drive."

Keeping Erna from ending up in the morgue was not a fun thing to do. I wished that Steffie minded her own business. Everything would run its course then—Sunday would come, and we wouldn't have a plan, and Mother would drag Erna along, and... oops!

But Steffie didn't let me forget. She nagged me almost constantly, and I began to wish that she had never come to visit. Finally, just to get her off my back, I called Paula to find out if she was going too, but Paula hadn't decided yet. She would let me know by Saturday.

Monday morning, Steffie went to the toilet across the hall. I was only half awake and hadn't looked at the clock yet. Suddenly, I heard a blood-curdling scream just as the door ripped open and Steffie came flying in. She was dressed in her favorite see-through baby doll pajama that might have fit her when she was ten. I looked at the clock and saw that it was just after eight. "Somebody saw you, huh?"

"Why didn't you tell me," she wailed as she hopped into bed and pulled the blanket way up to her nose.

"A guy?"

Steffie nodded.

"What did he look like?"

From Steffie 's description, I figured it must have been Herrmann from the sales department. Dreamy Herrmann with gorgeous black curls, dark brooding eyes, and an almost femininely beautiful face. Herrmann was so beautiful that his knock-knees never registered.

On Tuesday, Mother had us hang up the laundry on the flat roof of the warehouse again. We went by way of our attic from where another little iron bridge led to the flat roof. The last flight of stairs to the attic was so narrow, steep, and dark, that Steffie, who was following behind me, stumbled and dropped her end of the basket and all the clean laundry fell out. She was so mortified at seeing all that antique dust wiped away by the clean white laundry that she nearly fell off the stairs. Mother was not amused to find out that she had to do the laundry all over again. She remembered to put on her smile.

Wednesday morning, Steffie and I went to empty the garbage pail in the courtyard. The movie theatre doors stood wide open to air it out. We poked our heads through the heavy velvet curtains at the exit, and seeing the place empty we decided to explore it.

"See that little square door below the screen?" I explained. "I can remember seeing musicians coming out of it. They used to sit behind there and play for silent movies."

We scrambled through the little door, and there, in the dark, dusty space under and behind the screen we played Vulluvutz, monstrous creature of dark, until a shout disrupted the eerie silence. It was frumpy Fraeulein Hartung who said she would have to tell my parents. Yeah, go ahead and tell them, I thought. Hans gets numb all over from terrible headaches, Matthias still wets his bed at the age of five, Markus is clinging, shamefully, to his bottle at the age of four. Mother will be so impressed to hear what I did!

On Thursday, just as we came out of our room, Herrmann walked by. He slowed down, turned around, and smiled at Steffie. Her face turned red as a beet. She wanted to escape back into our room, but I had already locked the door. Not daring to turn to me for the key, she stood facing the door like a naughty child facing the corner. Herrmann,

94

grinning from ear to ear, took his sweet time before getting back to his work.

On Friday, we had to guard the kids who were playing on the flat roof. Of course there was a fence around it, but that had never stopped one or the other of us from climbing over it and onto the slanted roof of the house. Old lady Kraft had once reported me to Mother when I was having a grand old time on the snow-covered roof over the fourth floor, right above her apartment.

The kids wanted to play hide-and-seek in the warehouse. It was around five in the afternoon and the workers were leaving. We agreed to use the top three floors. Herrmann later told me that he had been watching for Steffie. He took customers to the warehouse from time to time, and on that Friday, he had heard us shouting and yelling on the roof and heavy leather shoes racing up and down the stairs inside the warehouse.

It was Hildegard's turn to seek, and the rest of us scurried into every direction, hiding in or under or behind the merchandize. Steffie had crawled behind a stack of stove-pipes. She told me later, that Herrmann had suddenly shown up beside her, and that she had been embarrassed and scared, and hot and cold, and wanting to escape and wanting to stay all at the same time. She had been so mixed up that she nearly wet her pants.

Hildegard never found Steffie, so we played a while without her. When I saw her later, I knew right away that something titillating had happened. She had an expression on her face that I had never seen before, and her grin was so big that it nearly jumped off her face.

"Tell me," I demanded after we had delivered the kids to Erna. Erna tried to get Mother to load me down with a few chores, but Steffie stood beside me, so Mother put on her smile and excused us.

Herrmann had tried to kiss Steffie, but she had managed to wriggle out of his reach. When he asked for her

95

address, she gave it to him. It didn't surprise me that he had made a hit with her. Herrmann made a hit with every girl who laid eyes on him, including Erna and Paula. They had tried to keep it a secret from me, of course. They referred to him as Helga whenever they openly talked about him in my presence. Thought I was stupid and not recognize their silly, giddy laughter, and the weird emphasis on the name, and the secretive looks on their faces.

"Has your sister Paula called yet?"

"No, not yet. I better call her right now."

Paula said she was going, too. She agreed that Erna, Steffie and I could drive with her and her husband. We were to be at her house by nine o'clock. As we left the apartment to go downstairs Steffie said, "you have to tell your mother that we're going with Paula."

Steffie was beginning to get on my nerves with her constant reminders of what I should do. That had always been my role, back in Venusbrunn. "Wait a minute. I think we better sort this out right now," I said and sat down on the steps. Steffie sat down beside me.

"And Sunday morning," she said, you coax Erna to our room where we'll tell her that she can't go."

I felt funny about this whole thing. I wasn't used to playing games with people. And to my surprise I realized that even though I didn't give a hoot about Erna, playing games with her life was beginning to worry me.

"I don't know," I stalled. "I'm gonna have to lie to Mother, and to Paula, and to Erna. They'll be mad as heck at me. And just how are we going to get Erna to come to our room?"

"You could tell her that you found the jewelry."

"And if she comes but doesn't believe this thing about your vision?"

"You could threaten to give away her secret. And maybe I should wait in the toilet with the room key. I could lock the door from outside so that she can't get away," Steffie plotted.

"Okay. And then you'll have to call Paula from the office and tell her that we're taking a second car after all and that she doesn't have to wait for us."

"Right."

We were hashing it out till long after we had gone to bed, kneading, and punching, and turning our plan like dough to make sure it would hold up under pressure. Yet, in the space between sleeping and waking I felt at odds with myself, as though my inner person and my outer person disagreed with each other. Did we really have the right to decide which way somebody's life should be headed? Then again, maybe the vision meant nothing at all.

I would think about it some more on Saturday, I promised myself. But then Mother forgot to put on her smile and hijacked us to the garden where we had to pick fruit and vegetables, buckets of it. Father did his share of the work by driving us and the full buckets home. Then we had to wash the stuff, and pit it, and peel it, and chop it, and grind it, and can it... Nevermind that we had planned to go swimming, or that a guest was being forced into slave labor. And nevermind that my fingernails, instead of getting a manicure for Sunday, got nasty black edges instead.

I did manage to tell Mother that Erna, Steffie and I would be riding with Paula and her husband. Mother told Erna, and Erna told me off for trying to control her life.

Throughout Saturday, a weird feeling kept poking its head into my preoccupation with chores. I never stopped wishing I had paid more attention to it. Perhaps Erna would still be alive.

Our plan worked like a charm. We locked the door on Erna and kept her from going to Maria Ehrenberg on that Sunday in July. After my family had left in our little

VW we let her go. Erna left the house, ranting and raving about being locked up in her very own room by a couple of idiots who tried to control her life.

I had forgotten that with the family gone, we wouldn't be able to get back into the apartment. There was nothing else to do but go to church, then walk around town, the castle grounds, and anywhere else I could think of that Steffie hadn't seen yet. We were getting hungry, but only had a bit of change for a small portion of ice cream from the Italian ice cream parlor in our neighborhood. I knew that Father could spend all day in the country eating lunch at a country restaurant, having afternoon coffee and cake at another, and on the way home he'd want to stop at his favorite country inn for cold-cuts and beer.

Not finding us with Paula, though, brought them home earlier. There was no smile on Mother's face when we stood before her. I could tell by her eyes, which were about to skewer me, just how furious she was that I had dodged her control. "Hogwash," was her comment to our explanation, and Father agreed. If it hadn't been for Steffie, Mother would surely have given the broomstick a workout on my bare legs.

She was right in the midst of a tirade about the evils of lying when Hildegard announced that a policeman was at the door. Mother and Father exchanged a few words with him while Steffie and I escaped down the long hallway to the kitchen. As I opened the kitchen door I could hear them all going into the study and shutting the door behind them.

My stomach was growling like mad. I collected bread, butter, and honey, and just as I started to spread the butter we heard Mother scream. Steffie and I looked at each other.

"What do you want on your bread? Jam or honey?" I asked.

"Honey is fine," Steffie said with a pensive little voice.

Hildegard came rushing into the kitchen with Markus and Matthias in tow. "What's the matter with Mom?"

"I don't know," I lied. My hands did their thing with bread and butter, but my mind was somewhere else, doing some other thing. Steffie was very quiet.

Father came in. One look at his face, and I knew what he knew. "Stef, you need to take care of the boys today," he said with a slow, somber voice.

"What's the matter with Mom?" Hildegard asked again.

"And I want you all to be very quiet today and don't disturb your mother."

"What's the matter with Mom?" Hildegard wailed.

That's when Father told us that Erna had been hit by a car.

Steffie had a crooked smile on her face and crooked cheerfulness in her voice when she said, "oh no. Erna is just fine. We saved her from that accident. That's why we kept her here, see?" Her smile wanted to wilt, but Steffie forced it to stay put.

"No, you don't understand," Father said. "She got hit by a car, here in town." I had never seen him so tired-looking, so very weary.

"But she'll be alright, won't she?" Hildegard asked, and her face and voice were such a mix of hope and fear that it made me want to cry.

"No, Hildy," Father said, and now he was fighting tears. "Erna died shortly after the accident." He turned to go back to Mother who had not come out of the study.

"Nooo!" Hildegard screamed. Hans had come into the kitchen just in time to hear that Erna was dead. He stared in disbelief, and Hildegard stared in disbelief, trying to digest the outrage of death having paid us a visit. Then Hildegard started to cry, and Hans asked questions that I couldn't answer, and Markus was getting cranky, and

99

Matthias whined, and I was so busy and so muddled that I didn't notice when Steffie left.

When I came downstairs later, her suitcase was packed. She sat on the sofa, stared straight ahead and didn't say anything for a long time.

"I wish I were just like everybody else," she suddenly mumbled as we unfolded the sofa.

"I guess you're stuck with it."

"It isn't fair," she said as we climbed into bed. "I thought I should try to save your sister." There was no emotion in her words. They were just statements.

"I guess it was meant to happen."

"I'm going home tomorrow," she said. "You'll be busy with the funeral and all that. I would only be in the way."

Steffie turned over and said no more. It took a long time before I dozed off. Between waking and sleeping I came to feel sorry for Erna and her short, sad life.

Steffie was still quiet when I took her to the railroad station and we said good-bye. She climbed on the train, sat down away from the window and did not look out. I waited till the train was out of sight, waving the whole time, but Steffie didn't wave back. I was sick with worry.

But I didn't have time to think about Steffie. With Erna gone, I was the one to look after the kids, and what a pain it was. Hans was only two years younger than I and didn't want to take orders from me. Hildegard had liked Erna a lot, and she cried all the time. Matthias sniveled, and Markus just didn't understand anything and just wanted to be with Mother. But Mother wouldn't come out of her bedroom. Thank goodness for aunt Elizabeth who was summoned to help out. Actually, she was not a real aunt to us but Father's sister's husbands' brother's wife's sister. But we liked her a lot, so we called her aunt.

On the day before the funeral Father and Mother went to the funeral chapel in the cemetery to view Erna's body. That afternoon, I had to take Hans and Hildegard to do the same. Hans didn't mind going inside, looking at Erna who was dead; he had a scientific curiosity about it all. But Hildegard refused to set foot in the funeral chapel. And she refused to stay alone outside the chapel; so many dead people, she complained. I knew she was scared. Hildegard had always been scared of all sorts of things: loud noise, shadows, the cellar, the creaky wooden stairs in the warehouse.

It was depressing, walking home from the cemetery with a sniveling child and a daydreamer on a warm, sunny day when the swimming pool beckoned and an ice cream cone. How very different from Christmas Eve afternoon when it was fun going to the cemetery to visit the silent members of the family. It was a somber ritual, but it was also filled with tingling anticipation of things to come.

The day of the funeral was sunny and hot. Long before the actual burial, the funeral chapel was full of people who said one rosary after another until the priest came to perform the burial rites. It was a large crowd that followed the coffin to the grave and it made the graveside service very long. My flat feet were hurting, my body wilted in the heat, my brain got fried by the sun. I stood by the back edge of the family plot with its tall gravestone, wishing I could cool my hot face on the cold marble. But I didn't dare to show such disrespect.

Just when I thought I could take no more, I was saved by a mouse. It poked its head out of a hole in the ground a few inches from me. It seemed totally oblivious to the still forest of legs around it and went about its little business, popping out of one hole, scurrying to another. Pretty soon, I had forgotten the funeral and poked my neighbor in the side to offer her a look at the cute little thing. My neighbor took one look, and instead of smiling appreciatively, she let out a scream and jumped back. The woman in back got stomped on her foot and screamed with pain. Throwing out her arms to catch herself, she hit her neighbors. The commotion rippled through the crowd of quiet mourners like rings on a still lake.

After the priest had done his thing and the coffin had been lowered into the ground, people dropped the flowers they had brought into the open grave. Then everybody dropped a little shovel full of earth into the grave. And when that was over a lot of people came and said their "Sorry" as they shook Mother's hand, and Father's hand, and Walter's hand, and Paula's hand, and my hand. I thought it would never end.

If Steffie and I hadn't kept Erna at home she would have gone to Maria Ehrenberg and still be alive today; that was the talk that permeated life, and if I didn't hear it out loud or whispered openly or in some corner then I heard it inside my head, day and night, anyplace I went. It was dreadful. It was useless to point to Steffie's vision. I should have known that my family wouldn't believe such "nonsense" anymore than Steffie's parents had at first. And now Erna was dead anyway.

I never dreamed that life could be worse without Erna. But it was. Mother was not used to showing any emotions, and Father was not used to comforting anyone. They became sullen with each other and more and more angry and impatient with the little kids. Even their boring dinner talk became ever more sparse. Then came silence, heavy with tension and ugly with grudging remarks.

I could hardly wait to get back to Venusbrunn.

All Saints Day, November first, fell on a Wednesday that year. Mother Superior had thought that it might be a waste of money to go home for just one day. We were to consult with our parents. The decision was unanimous; escape for one day was better than none.

I love a long train ride because strangers mind their own business and never interrupt my heavy thinking. Forgive yourself, Willie had said. But for what? For wishing to be rid of Erna? It was her own fault. She was out to ruin my life, and I should just sit there and take it? No, I figured, stomping down hard with the foot of my mind. She had been absolutely horrid to me, and I wanted her dead. It was a perfectly normal reaction. But it didn't work. I couldn't drown out the voice that kept whispering in the most unreachable place that I had no right.

The rhythmic clacking of train wheels running over rail joints replayed it relentlessly: no right.... no right.... no right.... I was on the second leg of my journey. Aschaffenburg would come next, and Wiesenthal, where Steffie lived, was not much farther. It would be very simple to get off in Aschaffenburg and take a train to Wiesenthal. It wouldn't cost much. Steffie would be so surprised. She had never written, had never called. She must be utterly miserable. It would be good to talk. We really needed to talk. Clack-clack..... no right..... clack-clack..... no right.....

When the train stopped I grabbed my suitcase and got off. I went to the ticket counter inside the depot. The next train for Wiesenthal would leave in fifteen minutes. Perfect timing. But I didn't have enough money for the ticket.

While I was trying to decide what to do, my train for Hanfurt left and the one to Wiesenthal rolled in on a different platform. I hurried down the steps and through the underground passage up the steps to the other platform and scrambled into the train. Once in my seat, I thought I'd play it dumb. If a conductor came to check my ticket, I would show him my ticket to Hanfurt. He would say that I was on the wrong train. Then I would jump up and wring my hands and shout in distress: "Oh no!" and maybe even squeeze out a tear or two. And he would suggest very kindly that I get off at the next stop. And that would happen to be Wiesenthal.

I didn't have a chance for dramatics, though, because the conductor never showed. I got out in Wiesenthal and asked directions to Steffie 's house. It turned out to be only four blocks from the station, down the street to the right. I was glad it wasn't raining. My heavy suitcase made me miserable enough, and not knowing what to expect from Steffie or her parents made me nervous.

It was around three in the afternoon when I got to her house, an old townhouse built of stone close to the sidewalk. It had two entrances, one to the apartments on the upper floors, and one door to her parents' photo shop on the ground floor. I found the doorbell with Steffie 's name on it and rang. Suddenly, a window flew open on the second floor and Steffie looked down with the most peculiar expression on her face. She seemed surprised and happy and glad and worried all at the same time.

"Stef!" she shouted and her eyes were big and her mouth stood wide open.

"Well, are you gonna let me in?"

She disappeared from the window. Then I heard heavy leather shoes thumping down a staircase and running across stone floor tiles, and then the door tore open and she flew around my neck and we hugged and laughed.

"Why didn't you let me know you were coming?"

"I didn't know. I just decided on the spur of the moment. Got out in Aschaffenburg and took a train here. That's it."

"You're coming from school?"

"Yep. All Saints Day tomorrow, you know."

"I'm glad you're here," she said pensively as we climbed the stairs to her apartment.

She took me to her room. It was a very nice room, girlish, ruffely, colorful, like some I had seen in fancy magazines. And she had it all to herself! Her parents were busy in the store, so we had time to talk.

"Do you want to call your parents and tell them you're not coming?"

"No. I never said I would."

"Then you must stay the night."

"Can I?"

Steffie was quiet for a moment. She looked thoughtful, sober. "I don't know," she admitted. "I never told my parents what happened, you know, with Erna. But they figured out that something went wrong. I came back earlier than planned, for one thing."

"And you never told them?"

"How could I. I can't even think about it."

"I know. I haven't talked about it either, except to Willi."

"How is Willi?" Steffie asked and her smile returned. I was glad to have something happy to tell her.

"Oh, he's so sweet, and so thoughtful, and so heavenly, and so.... so.... so...."

"Yeah, I know," Steffie said and laughed. "You don't need to say anymore."

"But he was sick one weekend and didn't come. And it was kind of strange how he mentioned it. He said that he got over it much quicker this time. It's like he's had the same thing before." I tried to remember the mood of that occasion. Steffie waited quietly. Suddenly, we heard someone coming toward the door.

"Quick," Steffie whispered and opened her wardrobe.

"Why? What's the matter?"

"Quick, get inside. I'll tell you later," she whispered urgently, pushed me into a thicket of clothes and shoved my coat in after me. Then she locked the wardrobe door.

I heard a noise, then someone came in; there were muffled sounds, then Steffie unlocked the door.

"It was my Mom. I have to get some groceries. You want to come along?"

"Sure. But why didn't you want your mother to know that I'm here?"

"Oh, I don't know. She'll want to talk to you and ask what happened at your house."

"So?"

"I don't want to talk about it."

"Steffie, I'll be here till Thursday. There's no bathroom in your wardrobe."

Steffie laughed. "I'll figure out something," she said. "Come on, we have to go."

The air was clear because her mother had gone back to the shop. It was beginning to get dark as we headed into the street with shopping net in hand. We bought milk and butter from the dairy shop, sausage from the butchery, and bread from the bakery. On the way back, Steffie pointed to a peculiar little building and said, "see that shop? That's Judith's."

The little shop was one in a whole block of houses that seemed to cling to each other for dear life. They were ancient things with leaning walls and worn-down stone steps, and great wooden doors that were tattered by centuries of weather and use. No two house-fronts were alike; some protruded, others sat back.

"Oh wow! I want to see what she sells," I said and pressed my nose against the window that was filled with a curious assortment of stones and crystals, and herbs, and books, and a bunch of other things I didn't even have a name for.

"Let's go in," I said and headed for the door. There was none. Steffie laughed.

"Where's the door?" I asked.

"Find it," she said with a giggle.

Although it was almost completely dark by now, I thought I should be able to see a door. But I couldn't. "There has got to be a door here somewhere," I said, getting annoyed and frustrated for not being able to find one. Steffie laughed all the more.

"This is ridiculous! How on earth does she make a living if people can't find the door to her shop?"

"She said that people who need her will find her," Steffie said, still laughing.

"All right, I give up."

Steffie grabbed my arm and led me to the end of the block and around to the backside of Judith's building. Above the door, lit by an ancient lamp beside it, was a sign that identified it as Judith's Shop of Metaphysics. Beside the door was an old-fashioned bell-pull.

"Let's go in, I want to see Judith," I said and grabbed the ancient ornate door handle.

"We don't have enough time. My Mom is waiting for the groceries."

"We can come back tomorrow. Oh darn it, All Saints Day. She won't be open."

"Well, let's just see," Steffie said and followed me inside.

A little bell tinkled as we opened the door. We came into a dimly lit corridor that led to the storefront. The place was crowded with stuff, too much to take in with just a glance. Behind the counter stood a plump woman of maybe forty, with wavy dark shoulder-length hair and a long, colorful, flowing dress.

She smiled warmly. "Hello Steffie. How are you?" she said. Her voice was soft, serene. It made me believe that nothing could disturb her composure.

"I'm fine, thank you. This is my friend Stef. Remember, I told you about her?"

"Yes I remember," Judith said and put down the papers she had been busy with. "What can I do for you?"

"Stef wants to... I mean, we both need to talk to you."

"You're in luck. My mother is here. She can mind the store while we talk."

"But we can't do it now," Steffie said. "I've got to get the groceries home. Will you be here tomorrow?"

"I'll be closed tomorrow. But how about Thursday?"

"I'll be in school and Stef has to leave."

"Wait, I don't have to leave till around noon. And you can skip school once, can't you? Could we come first thing in the morning?"

"Sure. Eight o'clock?"

"All right," I said and pulled Steffie with me out through the back door.

"I can't do it," Steffie protested as we headed back to her house. "I can't just not go to school."

"Why not? If you break a leg you can't go either, right? So you'll be a little late that morning. So what?"

Steffie sighed and said no more. I knew that she didn't want to talk about Erna, neither to Judith nor anyone else. But we all had to. It was the only way to get rid of the black cloud of guilt that had infected our lives. Besides, I wasn't about to give in to Erna who was six foot underground but had more power now than when she was alive.

To hide or not to hide, that was the question we debated on the way back to Steffie's house. She feared punishment or a scene. I was worried that her parents would call my parents and give me away.

"They won't snitch on you. My parents like you, remember?"

We couldn't decide how to handle it, so I just stayed out of sight in Steffie's room while she helped her mother do whatever they were doing. On her bed lay her bundle of stuffed animals that I knew from Venusbrunn, carefully, lovingly wrapped into what had been a baby blanket but was now just a rag. Pictures of animals on the walls, a lot of books on her bookshelf, junk on her desk - among it a letter from Herrmann.

"Wow!" I was toying with temptation, wrestling with my conscience, arguing with my Self; should I read it or shouldn't I?—Sure! We're friends— No, that's private— But we tell each other everything. Some things are off limits even to best friends. Darn it!

I was still holding the letter in my hand when Steffie came in. She lunged for it and yelled, "that's private!"

"Calm down! I didn't read it," I whispered. Steffie grinned from ear to ear and stashed the letter in one of her desk drawers.

"Can I read it?" It never hurts to ask, I firmly believe.

"No," she said like somebody who wants to have her secret coaxed out of her.

"Come on, you know you want me to read it."

"Alright. But don't you tell anybody what's in it, not even my mother, promise?"

"What is it? A marriage proposal?"

"Don't be stupid. It's nothing much. Promise?"

"Alright, I promise. But doesn't your mother know about it?"

"She knows I got the letter, but she doesn't know what's in it. She doesn't spy on me."

"Wow! My mother should take lessons from your mother," I mumbled, awed at so much privacy and privilege. Steffie took out the letter and handed it to me as if it were made of glass. It was a very nice letter that Herrmann had written only two weeks before.

"Nothing much, huh?" I said with surprise. "He's practically inviting you to go skiing with him."

"He's just saying that his family goes skiing and that he hopes to see me. What's the big deal?

"Hah! You're so naive! He'll probably stay overnight at the ski lodge, that's what."

"Okay, so I'm naive. Big deal."

"Will your parents let you go?"

"I don't know. But I have a lot of cousins and they all ski. I could always go with them."

It was after six o'clock and Steffie's father had closed the shop and came upstairs. My stomach clock rang dinnertime. Steffie had to go and set the table. I kept her door ajar and listened. I heard her Mother asking why she was setting the table for four. "We might have a guest," said Steffie calmly.

"Who?"

"My friend Stef from Hanfurt."

"Oh?"

"I invited her over All Saints Day; she could show up any time. It's okay, isn't it?"

"I don't mind, but I wish you had told me sooner. The stores are closed tomorrow and I might not have enough food on hand."

"Oh, I don't think you need to worry about that. She'll definitely get more to eat around here than she would at home with all those kids."

A few minutes later, Steffie rushed in, all a-giggle. "Put on your coat," she whispered. "I'm going to shut the kitchen door and the living room door. Then you can go downstairs and pretend you just arrived. Ring the downstairs bell. Now, wait till I get back."

I put on my coat, and when she gave me the go-ahead I grabbed my suitcase, went downstairs and rang the outside bell. Steffie came downstairs and we acted as if I had just arrived. She called for her mother and father, and they greeted me politely and said they were glad to see me. "Stephanie should have let us know you were coming. We could have picked you up at the station; you wouldn't have had to lug that heavy suitcase around," Steffie's mother said with a look of disapproval toward her. I felt like a cheating fool.

"Just in time for supper," Steffie's father said and suggested that I go and freshen up.

Supper seemed like the royal feast out of Beauty and the Beast. There were different breads, real butter, sausage and cheese. Steffie's parents pushed it all in my direction, insisting that I eat all I wanted. There was fruit and pastry, milk and juice, and they even offered to make hot chocolate for me. Such service! I wished I could stay forever.

"How is your family?" Steffie's mother asked. Steffie's head nearly fell into her dish. I was chewing on my bread, which gave me time to decide whether to tell the truth or be polite. Politeness won out. "Fine," I mumbled.

"I guess it was a little too much for your mother to have another person underfoot?"

"Oh no, not..," I blabbed without thinking.

"Oh yes, it really was," Steffie interrupted quickly. "I could tell it was too much for her. That's why I left early."

"I thought you came back early because you didn't want to do any more canning," Steffie's father said with a chuckle.

"Well, that too," Steffie admitted with a look of embarrassment.

We went to church the next morning, and then to the cemetery to remember the dead. I remembered Willi and his illness, and I resolved to ask him about it. I remembered Erna and the boyfriend who dumped her, and

111

the hidden jewelry, and wished that I could do things over. Steffie had her own regrets. I had never not talked so much in all my life as I did on that day. In fact, Steffie and I were so quiet that her mother began to worry about the condition of our health.

When the silence became too awkward, I said: "Steffie, we gotta talk."

"Why?"

"Because. I know you feel bad about Erna, but you shouldn't."

"Why not?"

"Because it was meant to happen, that's why." Steffie sat on the edge of her bed, her head drooping. Her dark curly hair hung around her face and concealed it. Her hands fiddled with her handkerchief.

"Stef," she said in her mousy little voice, still looking down as though she was afraid to look me in the eye. "You don't understand. In my vision, I never really saw Erna dead. I only saw her getting hit. You see what I'm saying?"

"Oh, wow! You mean we kind of jumped to the conclusion that she was dead, and maybe she wasn't?" Steffie nodded, looking at me with sad eyes that begged forgiveness.

I felt so bad. To watch Steffie flounder in such misery was almost too much to bear. I didn't know what to say, so I hugged her.

"You know, I feel pretty guilty myself. My whole family made me feel guilty. But Willi said that I feel guilty because I wished Erna dead. He said that thoughts have power."

"He's right. I've seen it. I was really mad at my cousin one day and I wished something bad would happen to her. Those thoughts made a thought form, a really weird, ugly looking thing, and it hovered over her and then she got real mad. She was so mad that it scared me."

"You know, I kept wondering why I feel so guilty, and I don't think it's just because I wished her dead. I mean, she was really nasty to me, and I'm not a saint, just a kid-sister. But maybe it's because I should have listened to me instead of somebody else."

"Like me, you mean."

"Yeah. Maybe I should have done what I thought was right even if it turned out wrong. At least I wouldn't have to blame myself for doing something I didn't want to do in the first place."

"Do you hate me for it?" Steffie whispered, her head sinking ever deeper.

"No! Of course not! Is that what you were thinking? Is that why you didn't call or write?"

Steffie looked up and nodded pensively.

"I could never hate you," I said and hugged her. She gave a sigh of relief, and we agreed it would be good to hash it all over with Judith. Eight o'clock sharp.

The bell tinkled again as we came through the door. I headed down the corridor with Steffie and her school bag in tow. She wanted to chicken out of seeing Judith again, complained that she couldn't afford missing math, worried that she'd get in trouble with the teachers. But I knew what had to be done.

Judith was waiting for us. She disappeared behind a curtain for a moment, and then came back with an older woman. She had that same serene composure about her that I had noticed on Judith. She motioned Steffie and me down the narrow hallway that we had come through, and into a room that was decorated with all sorts of symbols and figures, pictures and posters and objects that were all very strange to me. A peculiar but not unpleasant odor permeated the little room.

"What is this?" I whispered to Steffie. "A tomb? A museum? A temple?

"Shut up," she whispered back with a giggle.

Judith sat down behind a table and motioned us to sit down in a couple of chairs that were facing her. She had a smile that was warm, and sincere, and patient, as though she had nothing more important to do than listen to a couple of girls. "Tell me what happened."

"How did you know anything happened?" I asked. Then I saw the little crystal ball in her hand. Steffie had told me about it. Judith was holding it by a short chain, and it was swinging back and forth.

"I get my information directly from Spirit," she said gently.

"Spirit what?" I asked, proud of myself for demonstrating such discerning intelligence.

"The same Spirit that animates all of us," she replied with a knowing smile. Exit my discerning intelligence.

Steffie started telling, or rather, she started hemming and hawing. When I lost patient I butted in and told all, from the start. Judith didn't seem shocked about what happened to Erna. With much compassion in her voice, she said to Steffie, "you feel guilty, don't you."

Steffie nodded, hardly daring to raise her eyes off the floor.

"You feel guilty," Judith said with emphasis on the word feel. "But are you?"

"Well, Erna is dead, and she died in Hanfurt because we didn't let her go to Maria Ehrenberg."

"How do you know that she died because and not despite your interference?"

"I don't, really. But maybe she wouldn't have died on the mountain. I never actually saw her dead."

"Visions are a tricky thing, Steffie. They come to us from a different level of existence, and because they have to make it through our physical brains, there is plenty of room for distortion."

114

With mouths gaping, we sat and stared at her.

"It's as if you had to translate a text from Russian to German. Do you know Russian?"

Steffie grinned and shook her head.

"Suppose you had to do it anyway."

Steffie fidgeted in her chair like a child caught at some mischief. "I guess I'd have to make up something. Anything."

"But the words would be German words, because that's what you know, wouldn't they?"

Steffie nodded.

"And how accurate, do you think, this translation would be?"

"It would be all wrong," Steffie said and laughed at the thought of such nonsense. "And that's what my brain did when it translated that vision?"

"That's right."

"So, the vision might not have anything to do with Erna at all?"

"True. The physical brain is trying to make sense out of that vision from the higher plane, and it does it with the symbols that it knows."

"Stuff that I know about, or can understand?"

"That's right."

"But wait a minute," I butted in. "Steffie had never seen my sister before the vision. So how could Erna be in it?"

"Sometimes, we get little glimpses of the future, or the past, for that matter. That could explain Erna in the vision before Steffie had seen her. There are so many states of existence, and so many different forms of clairvoyant experiences — hearing, seeing, intuiting, of the future and the past — that anything is possible."

I figured that it must be something like living on five different continents in the past, present and future, all at the same time.

"Next time you have a vision like the one you described, dear, pray for that person and send her helpful and loving thoughts. That's the best that anyone can do."

"And she's not guilty of anything, right?" I said firmly. I wanted Judith to say it, out loud, so that Steffie could hear it.

"It's not quite that simple," Judith said. "You are both guilty for interfering in someone else's life even though you meant well. You don't know what kind of Karma Erna had to work out. By interfering, you might have altered that process.

"What's Karma?" I asked.

"It is the natural law of cause and effect. Everything you do, and even what you think, has consequences. Suppose Erna incurred a debt in a previous life, and suppose she was going to work it out in this life—by interfering in her life you may have prevented her from accomplishing that task."

"Oh, that's were the many lives come in that Steffie had told me about, right?"

"That's right. And through this interference in Erna's life you have created some Karma for yourself, which you will have to work out sooner or later," Judith said, and her voice and smile were just as loving and kind as if we had done a saintly thing.

"There is never only one option, you know. We do have choices, and according to our choices, so will events develop. There is no right or wrong answer, just different choices with different outcomes. Erna will have many more lives. We all do. We have lessons to learn and we have all eternity to do it. But Steffie, the next time you feel you must help, do it by warning the person in question. He may not listen, and you may be sorry you opened your mouth—that's the price you pay—but let him have a choice. Don't decide for him. It deprives him of the freedom to make his own choices."

"See?" I said to Steffie. "That's just what I thought: I should have had a choice, too. I should have decided for myself."

Steffie looked relieved, and even a little happy. But she stayed put on her chair as though there was more. She repeated some things that Judith had said, rephrased some others, gave me a funny look. Judith waited patiently. I had all morning.

"There's something left undone," Judith coaxed.

"What?" Steffie asked, looking to Judith. But Judith said nothing, just smiled and waited. Steffie thought about it some more. Suddenly, she lifted her head and said: "What about Stef's parents?"

"What about them?" Judith asked.

"Well... I feel like I have to do something. Or say something."

"Willi said I should forgive myself."

"That's it. I have to ask your parents for forgiveness," Steffie said haltingly, her face cutting a sour grimace.

"But you're not guilty of anything," I protested.

"We lied. We forced Erna to stay," Steffie said. She was right, of course. I knew that I would have to do the same thing. We looked at each other and grinned, and knowing that we shared the same sour task took some of the sting out of it.

"And don't forget to forgive yourself," Judith added, as we got up to leave. "Carrying around a rock on your shoulder is deadly." There was that same warm smile on her face that made me feel so good. "Could you please wrap up that smile for me, so I can take it home?" I asked as Steffie laughed and yanked me by my coat sleeve out the door. "Your mother has too many kids and too much work," she said. As if I didn't know.

We practically ran all the way to Steffie's school. Her voice lesson was one lesson she didn't want to miss.

The school was housed in an ancient building that had once been a monastery. It was dark and gloomy and its walls were shell-damaged from the war. We hugged, promised to write, and then she disappeared through a large portal into the courtyard.

Since I had plenty of time and I loved to explore, I took a long, roundabout way back to Steffie 's house. I saw one bomb crater, a couple of shelled houses, but nothing like Hanfurt. Her parents showed me around their photo shop, which included an apprentice and a journeyman. Afterward, Steffie's mother took me upstairs, fixed me some sandwiches to take along and invited me to come visit again. I said good-bye, picked up my suitcase and took off.

Trudging back to the station, it suddenly occurred to me that I had nothing but dirty laundry in my suitcase. And no laundry services till Christmas! I had two choices: I could run around in dirty underwear for the next six weeks—disgusting! Or, I could spend the coming Saturday afternoons doing my laundry by hand and missing out on seeing Willi. What a choice!

All the way back to Venusbrunn, Judith's words kept fluttering through my head the way emotions flutter through my stomach. Amidst the muddle of thoughts a letter to my parents grew, sentences formed, rearranged themselves, words to Willi snug in and others bowed out, but the muddle only grew. I was exhausted by the time I got to bed, yet sleep was hard to come by.

Sometimes, in the space between waking and sleeping, tears would rise in my eyes, but I never knew why. But Spirit knew. Spirit always knows. It knew that Willi would die. And once in a great while for just an instance, I knew too. But this knowing flashed by so quickly that it was gone before my mind could get a good grip on it. So I never learned what Spirit knew until it was too late.

I got back to boarding school after Christmas vacation of my third year, expecting the weeks till Easter to be dull, tiresome, and utterly boring – until I discovered a new face among the familiar ones.

The face was gorgeous. It had ravishing green eyes, the complexion of a movie star, a cute little nose, and a halo of platinum blond curls. To make matters worse, this gorgeous face belonged to an equally gorgeous body, with all the proper bulges and hollows in all the right places. Made me feel like a flagpole - straight, skinny, and hopelessly outclassed.

Inge, that was her name, sat across from me at breakfast. Her teeth were perfect, too. She was looking toward Mother Superior who was standing at the head of the table. Her speech impressed no one that morning. All eyes were on Inge, and Inge knew it. She expected to be stared at; her smile said as much. She had tied her platinum blond curls in a ponytail, which revealed a pair of delicate little ears. She wore a dress, not a drab, sensible school dress such as mine but a dress for showing-off. It was red, had a tight bodice, and a V-neck that showed cleavage. The skirt was tight and short; it barely covered her knees. She wore no apron.

Mother Superior stood tall and powerful like a man, her thumbs tucked into her wide belt across her broad middle. Then came the familiar fascinating interplay of mustache and mouth that I found so fascinating. Finally, with a few sparse words she introduced Inge to the rest of us. Gusti whispered to Inge, "why in the middle of the last year?"

"Oh, because....," she said with a short, tinkly laugh.

"You'll be way behind in English," I pointed out.

"I'll manage," she said with a patronizing smile. Then she sat back and looked around to see how many eyes were on her.

I had to admit that Inge looked captivating. I couldn't help staring at her, despite the mounting envy. I summoned all the confidence I could muster and fluffed up my self-image to relieve that awful sensation of inadequacy; but the stunning looks from across the table bedeviled my valiant efforts. Yet there was something about her face.....

After breakfast, Sister Fallada approached Inge. She had that look on her face, the look she had when she told me I couldn't dress up as a guy for our Carneval dance; and she had it when she told Mechtild she shouldn't spend so much time with little, adoring Janni from the eighth grade. With her beady little eyes shooting darts from behind her glasses, Sister informed Inge that aprons were in and cleavage was out.

Sister Harmony had begun our German lesson when Inge, plus apron and minus cleavage, waltzed in. She looked around the classroom, and when she was satisfied that all eyes were on here she said loudly, "I'm Inge Schoenlein. Where do I sit?"

Sister Harmony mustered her with obvious displeasure. Sister had a soft, flabby face with soft fleshy lips that she moved in a fascinatingly icky way. Her head always tilted to the right, and her roof-shaped headgear tilting with her head made it look like she was about to fall over. She had a sour disposition, no sense of humor, and no sense of fun. Besides German, she taught bookkeeping and business math.

"I'm Sister Harmony," she said, held up a book for Inge to take and pointed to an empty seat in my row. Inge strode to it in the most conspicuous way possible, picking up the book on the way. She sat down beside me with one empty seat left between us. Then, leaning way over to me, she whispered loudly, "eeny, meeny, miny, more, Sister's gonna hit the floor."

I cracked up laughing. In view of Sister's hateful look, though, I got myself under control quickly. Sister Harmony didn't like me. I was not like my sister Erna who had excelled in bookkeeping and business math. Sister took it very personal.

We took turns reading an epic poem about the early Germanic tribes. It was full of archaic words and bizarre culture and unreal people. My mind kept wandering to Willi whom I hadn't seen in almost four weeks. Today was Monday, and I would have to wait five long days before I would look into his wonderful blue eyes again.

"Stephanie! Daydreaming again?" Sister's voice tore into my romantic fantasy. "Maybe your parents should have kept you at home after that escapade of yours. You're not learning anything here. Read now."

I felt her words like a sting. I read, but I didn't hear much. My mind escaped to the park with its grand old trees and strange sensation, and to the old mill at the edge of town that I knew and didn't know. Sister's hateful remark hadn't faded away with her voice; it remained suspended in the classroom. I had long felt isolated and alone in a space to which no one had entry but Willi. There were moments when I envied the other girls who seemed so happy with their boyfriends and latest fashions and hairstyles, who were witty and clever, who seemed to know what was going on in the world and always were sure of themselves. But my lonely space was precious to me. Everything

121

outside of it, I sensed, would not fit me.But since Willi hat entered I was happy.

Inge hoarded everyone's attention including mine. She did weird things, like changing her clothes in the middle of the day. She monopolized the mirrors, talked incessantly about clothes, hairdos, and make-up, and she laughed at my braids and knee-high socks. Every day, she put on a different dress, and every day, Sister Fallada sent her back to change. Pretty soon, Inge refused to change. She said it was embarrassing to wear the same dress for a whole week, and she looked us up and down like a drill sergeant musters his troops.

"Why does she get away with stuff like that?" Mechtild wanted to know. "And how come she doesn't get in trouble?"

"Never mind," Sister Angela said soothingly.

"Why?" Ellen piped up. "Who is she? The Duchess of Special Privilege?"

"That is quite enough. You just see to your own behavior and leave Inge alone. She has had enough trouble as it is."

"What kind of trouble?"

"That is not your business," Sister replied and walked off.

Every chance she got, Inge put on this little act about traveling to Rome, Italy. She had been to Rome, the Holy City, with her parents, and the nuns were much impressed by the fact. She rehashed the same dumb incidents in a silly fake Italian accent over and over again until Gusti said, "Inge, shut up!"

"You're just jealous because you didn't get to go to Rome," Inge replied, and with another one of those up-and-down-looks she turned her back on us.

Once Inge got tired of keeping her own company she attached herself to me. Heaven only knows why. She made fun of me, my braids, my clothes. I didn't care, though, until Saturday rolled around, and it began to dawn on me that my attachment might want to follow me to Cafe Pole where I had a long-standing date with Willi.

"Are you going to confession?" she asked me that morning at breakfast.

"Yes," I said without thinking.

"You mean, you actually go to confession?"

"Of course," I lied.

"Just what do you confess? Monday I lie, Tuesday I steel, Wednesday I kill Sister Harmony?"

"It's not funny. There are all sorts of sins, mortal sins and subtle ones," I remarked, feeling anxious for committing the ultimate sin of fraternizing with a boy.

A big smile spread over Inge's face. That's when I realized what a dumb thing I had done. Inge would want to go to town and hang out with me. I could have kicked myself for being so stupid.

Throughout the morning, I tried to convince her that I wasn't going after all. I coughed an occasional cough, dabbed my nose with my hanky from time to time, added a sniffle for extra measure. By lunchtime, I mentioned that I wasn't feeling very well.

When time came, the other girls left, and Inge followed them. I waited a few minutes and then grabbed my coat, and just as I set foot outside the door I could see her waiting down the street. She stood on the opposite sidewalk near the bend in the street. Quickly, I pulled back inside, hoping she hadn't seen me. Sister Fallada walked by, mcasurcd me with her beady little eyes. "I forgot something," I said and headed for the little shoe-room beside the front entrance.

Willi wouldn't just leave if I didn't show up on time, I knew. But I didn't want to lose a single minute with him. I checked through the window; Inge was still waiting. Five minutes later, she was still there. I was getting desperate.

Across the street lay the construction site for the new high school. I knew I'd be out of her view if I could just make it to the far sidewalk. When Inge turned her face away I dashed across the street and onto the construction site. Among piles of building equipment and earth I worked my way to an alley, then down a side street until I hit the main street right near Cafe Pole. Just as I breathed a sigh of relief, Inge came around the bend in my direction. I pretended not to see her and hurried toward the Cafe. I walked past it, turned into a narrow winding side street that led to the church and hid in the entrance to a courtyard. A minute later, Inge showed up, stopped for a moment to look down the side street and then went on. I breathed a sigh of relief, snug back to the Cafe and rushed inside.

Willi was sitting at our favorite table in the back. He saw me coming, and if my stomach hadn't been in turmoil already, his sweet smile would have surely done me in.

"Been waiting long?" I asked as I sat down opposite Willi. I was trying hard to stop the awful flutter in my stomach.

"I got here early," he replied with a shrug, but his gorgeous blue eyes only increased my flutters.

"I had to lose an attachment," I explained. Willi looked puzzled. "We have a new girl, and she wanted to come with me."

"Funny, funny," he said with a grin. Then he laid his arms across the table in my direction and opened his hands toward me like an invitation. I put my cold hand into his warm hands, and we looked into each other's eyes. That's when I felt the tears rising.

The waitress came to take our orders, and the interruption gave me a chance to stow away those annoying tears.

"What happened?" Willi asked when the waitress had left.

"What do you mean?"

"You looked like you were going to cry."

"Oh, it's nothing," I said. Willi waited. "Sometimes, I think I'm actually two people, the one you can see, and another one on the inside who does stupid stuff. But we better not talk about it or I'm going to start again."

There was an awkward silence; then we said a few things, silly stuff, like fishermen who throw out bait and hope for a bite. Willi took his wallet out, and from it he pulled the photo of me that I had given to him. "Look at it," he said. "It's all worn out. You better get me a new one."

"I can beat that," I said, and reaching from under the lower edge of my sweater into my meager cleavage and produced Willi's cracked and frazzled photo. Willi grinned.

"I don't know where to put it. Can't carry around a wallet. Besides, this is the safest place."

I had just stowed away the photo in its original place when the waitress came with our goodies. Of course, she knew Willi, and of course, she knew I belonged to the convent. Judging from her smile, though, I figured that she was on our side. Willi said, "what you need is a locket. Then you can carry me around with you."

Right near my heart, I wanted to say, but I stopped myself from committing such mush.

"I really like being with you," Willi said and got me so flustered that I was glad to have a piece of cake to attack.

"I like you too. You're not like other guys," I replied, and cake crumbs fell from my munching mouth.

"What are other guys like?" Willi asked with a sly grin as if he already knew but wanted to hear it from me.

"Oh, they're silly.... making fun and teasing all the time. Everything's a big joke to them. You can't have a decent conversation, you know? You should know. You're a guy."

"That's what my mother tells me," Willi said, and it made me laugh. "But how do you know so much about guys? Do you have a boyfriend in Hanfurt?"

"No, I don't. Just the guys from my Dad's business; they always want to flirt. But you're not like them. You're different."

"What makes me different?"

"You're quiet, and ...." The word I wanted to use rang awfully corny in my mind, but it was the right word, a perfect word for what I wanted to say. I gave myself a mental shove, and with a forceful nod of my head I came out with it, "and you're gentle and kind." Willi grinned self-consciously. "And you know a lot of interesting stuff, like gnomes and elves. Can you see any right now?"

Willi looked around. He pointed to a table near the window. The sun was shining on it. "See that table? There are three little sun fairies; they slide down the sunbeams, and after they hit the table they dance a little jig. Then they fly up the sunbeam and come sliding down again. They're having a ball."

"They must be so cute! I wish I could see them."

"And your own little fairy, Georgette, is sitting right there, on your right shoulder, watching everything we do. But she won't give us away," Willi said with a look of collusion toward the little fairy.

"How about your little Otto? What's he up to?"

The smile on Willi's face wilted. "Oh, not much these days...."

I loved to watch him talk. There was something very steady, mature about his face. But something was also different. It seemed to me that his face had lost its rosy baby glow. He looked pale, or skinny, or something. Of course, it was winter, and my suntan had faded, too. He wore a plaid flannel shirt and a knitted vest over it. His blond hair was freshly cut and sleeked back with great care.

126

"You're in the twelfth grade now, right?" I asked, feeling elated to think that Willi, only one year away from philosophy studies at the university, thought enough of me to care about his appearance.

He nodded. "I'm in the Unterprima. – How was Christmas?"

I told him. I told him about my pesky little sisters and brothers, and my snobbish sister Paula who had married a business man and was expecting a baby, and about the crown prince of Hanfurt, my brother Walter, who thought he was king already, and my Father's hardware store, and my Mother's huge garden, and how, for some strange reason, there's always somebody sick on Christmas Eve.

Willi nodded thoughtfully. He was quite tall, but during my lengthy monologue he had begun to slump. The rosy baby glow was definitely missing from his cheeks. "You haven't been sick, too, have you?" I asked.

"Oh, just the same old thing," he replied. I had heard that from him before, I remembered.

"What's wrong with you?"

"Nothing much. Just the kidneys acting up when the weather gets cold." He flashed a smile that was meant to pacify, and it worked because I didn't pay the right attention. "What are you going to do after graduation?" he asked, and I talked about me, me, me...

Leaving Willi to go back to the convent was always a queer thing. Happiness lit up my face like a Christmas tree while fear of discovery plagued my insides. Venusbrunn was small enough that everybody knew everybody else. Boarding students stood out like sheep of a different color. If it got back to Mother Superior where I went for confession she'd swoop down on me with punishment that would surely include house arrest. If that prospect wasn't bad enough, there was always the word of authority from the Gospel about life being a valley of tears. It was enough to turn on optimist into a pessimist.

I got back in time for afternoon coffee, which was followed by study time. I hurried to exchange my shoes for house slippers and then went to the dining hall. I was worried. I didn't know what to expect from Inge. She was already there, and the others were coming in one by one.

At first, she said nothing. Just looked me over from top to bottom. That, I felt, must be what it's like to lie spread out on the butcher's block. Then, with her green eyes boring holes into my hide, and with heavy emphasis on every word, she hissed loudly, "I though you weren't feeling well."

"I'm not," I said and coughed for emphasis.

"You said you weren't going to confession."

"I changed my mind."

"You feel sick but still go to confession? Such devotion," she sneered.

"Shhh," I whispered, seeing Sister Angela heading our way. When she was out of earshot, Gusti said to Inge, "you have to know something, Inge - Saturdays are for confession. But there are no rules about who to confess to. We want to keep it that way. Right?"

The girls who sat close enough to hear laughed. Inge caught on right away, and a huge grin spread across her flawless face. I was relieved.

"Well, let's go to confession together next week," Inge said, winking at me. Her eyes were wide with expectant excitement, and her nodding head set her platinum blond curls in bouncing motion. I was spreading jam on my bread and nearly dropped the knife.

"Oh, I don't think she'd like that," Mechtild said with a short laugh and a significant look in my direction.

"Why not?" Inge asked.

"Because confessions are private, silly goose," Mechtild replied and laughed again, and everybody who had heard joined in. I was horrified to see that my secret was no secret at all.

"Whatever are you laughing about?" I asked, pretending innocence. I felt it would be wise to practice denial skills in case Mother Superior should ever find out. I'd be better prepared to weather the storm.

"Oh, don't you know yet that you can't keep secrets around here?" Mechtild quipped.

"Well, maybe we could if you minded your own business," I hissed at her.

"Well look, you don't need to worry about me," Inge whispered across the table with a tinkly laugh. "I'm perfectly capable of keeping secrets." Her tinkly laugh suffered a crack. And there was that something about her face again...

Two days later, Marlies learned that her older brother had died in a motorcycle accident on an icy road. Her parents came by car to take her home for the funeral. The rest of us girls sat together that evening in the classroom, which served as living room the rest of the day. We were knitting, or crocheting, talking about the brothers we all had. I held the record with four brothers. The mood changed from somber to relaxed to absolutely silly when Gusti and Mechtild began telling their brothers' shenanigans. I noticed that Inge who sat on my right hadn't said a word.

"Do you have any brothers?" I asked her. Not that I cared a whole lot. I just wanted to make her feel part of the group.

Inge didn't reply. I figured she hadn't heard and repeated the question, pushing at her with my shoulder to get her attention. "Don't touch me!" she yelled and moved farther away.

"All right, all right, I won't touch you," I said, feeling like a leper.

Ellen asked, "well, do you have any brothers or not?"

Inge mumbled something unintelligible.

"Yes or no?"

"Who cares," she snapped and stormed out of the room.

"Well, she either has diarrhea or she hates brothers," Roswitha said.

A few minutes later, I went looking for her in the toilet room. It was the only place to go; everything else was locked up. She stood by the open window and stared at the moon. It was much too cold to be standing by an open window. "Better come inside," I said. "You'll catch cold." I went back to the classroom. So she didn't have diarrhea. Must be the subject of brothers that got her so irate. Hmm…

"She's standing by the open window, trying hard to catch her death of cold," I reported to the others.

"Why do you care about her anyway?" Mechtild wanted to know. "She's nothing but a nuisance. You can't believe a word she says. She'll snap at you for nothing. She's got nothing interesting to say."

"And she brags a lot," Helga added.

"Oh, I don't know," I said. "Maybe I feel sorry for her. I wonder what her problem is."

"Problem? What could be her problem? She has everything she could want: great looks, perfect body, gorgeous hair and even travel. Why would you be sorry for her?" It was Roswitha who put in a rare comment.

"I'm not sure," I said. "But there is something about her that puzzles me."

No talking was the rule for bedtime. No talking in the washroom, no talking in the bedrooms, no talking in hallway or toilet. But Inge talked incessantly that night. She jabbered on about how her previous teachers had admired her beautiful voice and high I.Q. She bragged about her vacations in sunny Italy, and her rich uncle's exotic gifts from his African safaris, and her other uncle's friendship with the Bishop. She claimed that her mother knew the Prince of Leuchtenberg who was Godfather to mad King Ludwig of Bavaria. She went on and on, and it began to look as though she forgot where reality ended and imagination began. She rattled on right in front of Sister Angela who stood guard in the washroom, on a spot from where she could observe almost every girl at her assigned basin. She had her eyes lowered modestly, her hands working a rosary, her lips moving in silent prayer—probably afraid to see too much flesh. When she did spot someone in a slip that showed some cleavage the culprit had to cover up.

Inge jabbered on that night, and Sister could not shut her up, not with kind words, not with threats. It was as if Inge talked to keep herself from doing something else. Punishment, I was sure, would follow swiftly. I hoped that Inge would be sent to the dungeon to pick aphid-infested sprout-worms off the old potatoes.

When Sister Fallada headed for our table at breakfast I was gloating inwardly. I nearly went into shock, though, when I discovered that Sister had come for me instead. She hauled me to the courtroom. Willi, I thought. They found out about Willi. My stomach was sick with fear and anxiety while my mind rehearsed lies. Anything to keep my Saturday freedom.

It was a relief when Mother Superior finally came in, all three of her - judge, jury, and executioner. To my surprise, she didn't roar at me at all but sat down at the table instead. She attempted a friendly smile, but it turned into a grotesque grin. Then followed some polite chitchat about my family and my sister Erna who had come before me. I had never revealed to the nuns that Erna had died in an accident the previous summer. Now I was forced to make up stories about Erna who, as a graduate, was presumed to be living happily ever after.

My attention was totally absorbed by the contortions of Mother Superior's mouth. I almost missed the point of this weird visit; she wanted me to look after Inge. Inge, she said, had had some trouble in her life, and what she needed was a good friend. Would I be willing to be a friend to Inge?

What was this trouble, I wondered. Did it have anything to do with brothers, I didn't dare ask. I feared that my guilty conscience might trip me up. Mother Superior didn't volunteer any other information.

It couldn't hurt to be cooperative, I figured. Might even help me out later, if the nuns found out that I had broken the number one taboo. Inge had already attached herself to me anyway. So, I agreed.

When Saturday rolled around again, Inge said with a smile that felt as unnerving as if she were reading my private mail, "does your Father Confessor have a good-looking friend?" The laugh that followed made me want to stuff it down her throat.

"I don't know any."

"Oh, come on now," she pried.

"I don't. I don't care about guys." It was the absolute truth. I only cared about Willi.

"Oh sole mio, I don't believe you." She belted it out so loud that Sister Angela came traipsing in our direction.

"Look, let's talk about this later. The walls have ears," I whispered across the table.

"A little less noisy, please," Sister Angela said soothingly as she walked by.

I tried to think of a way to keep Inge away. Sister Harmony complained that I was daydreaming. I stared out the window, trying to fasten my eyes to some big old trees. But there were none. Heaps and lumps and piles of all shapes and sizes marked the unfinished landscape of the new high school across the street. Work had stopped. A light snow was falling.

By the time Sister Harmony left the classroom for recess, I knew what to say to Inge, "look, my Saturday afternoons are for me and myself. Get it?"

Inge said nothing.

"I'm willing to be your friend, but Saturday afternoons are off limits."

Inge kept quiet, looked straight ahead.

"Why don't you go to the library. With your looks you'll stir up some cute guys in no time at all."

That seemed to do it. As if she had known it all along but temporarily forgotten, she suddenly straightened up, confident in the knowledge that I was right.

"We can leave here together, but when we get downtown, we split up, okay?"

"All right."

We were putting on our coats and shoes when Sister Fallada remarked about my great devotion to confession. The smirk on her face gave me the jitters. Any second now, I feared, she would lower the boom and I'd be banned from Willi forever. My stomach began to squirm with nasty squiggles, and it didn't calm down until we were well out of sight of the convent.

We passed Cafe Pole on our way to the library, which stood at the edge of the town square together with a hotel, four hundred year old city hall, a butcher shop, two bakeries, an Apothecary, and a dairy shop.

The light snow cover of the morning had vanished. The cobblestones glistened with moisture and were slippery to walk on.

"You don't really think I'm going to spend my free time in there, do you?" said Inge with disdain.

"What else are you going to do?"

133

"I don't know yet, but I'll think of something." She looked around the square like someone looking for trouble. I decided to take off before she glued herself to me.

I got to the cafe before Willi. I didn't like getting there first because I never knew if Willi was sick again and would not show up. Then I'd be tormented by doubting and hoping, doubting and hoping, talking myself into believing he would come because it was what I wanted, and talking myself out of believing he would come because it would hurt so much if he didn't. The tension in my stomach would make me nearly ill.

But Willi came this time, out of breath from running all the way from his house. He'd been doing homework and nearly lost track of time. His disheveled hair and glowing cheeks made him look adorable.

"Do songs ever make you cry?" he asked straight out as he sat down opposite me, his face one big smile. I knew that smile. It was the kind that defied all attempts at controlling it, as if it originated somewhere outside the body instead of inside it. There was no hiding any feelings then. Might as well be broadcasting.

"I don't know," I said, startled by this unexpected question.

"Like the one about evening in the heath, and the poet who yearns for his lost love. You know that one?"

"Do I know it! Just thinking about it could make me cry. You too?"

Willi nodded. "Just don't ever tell anybody. If it got back to the guys, I'd never hear the end of it."

The waitress took our orders. "But why is it that we feel like crying when we hear that song? Oh, I can think of another one. The one about the mill in the hollow, and the sweetheart that didn't wait for her lover to return, and the ring she had given him that broke in two? It reminds me of that old mill right here in Venusbrunn."

"What mill?"

134

"That's just what I call it. It's that old building on the road to Wolkmann mountain. It looks like it might have been a mill."

Willi's eyes lit up. "Yeah, I know which one you mean. It really was a mill at one time."

"You want to know something weird? I could swear that I know it even though I've never been here before."

"Do you have any feelings about it?"

"Sure do. I feel sad about it, as if I had lost something there. And I feel the same way in our park, by those big old trees." I had gotten quite excited by now, and noisy. Willi laid his hand on mine.

"You might have lived here in a previous life," he said. "And maybe that's why you cry when you hear that song about the mill—maybe it was this one! And maybe that's why you wanted to come to Venusbrunn to go to school here in the first place. Did you ever think about that?"

"No, I never have. Oh my goodness! It would mean that Steffie and Judith were right!"

"My Mom says that certain things can conjure up scenes from past lives. For us it's these songs, for you it's also a place, for other people something else."

"But wait a minute! You said that the song about the mill makes you cry, too. Why?"

"Maybe we had similar experiences. Maybe you and I," — Willi's face almost glowed as he talked— "Maybe you and I have been together before; maybe we were lovers then, and maybe something sad happened to us."

At the word lovers I felt a hot sensation creeping into my face. I didn't know which way to turn my eyes.

"Could be that..." Someone suddenly appeared at our table. I looked up and was shocked to see Inge standing there. She looked from Willi to me and back to Willi, and

135

the grin on her face made me want to kick her butt to kingdom come.

"Well, hi there," she chirped and grinned and bounced her platinum blond curls. Her eyes glued to Willi, she said, "what a cute Father Confessor."

Willi looked confused, then he looked pleased, then he looked utterly enchanted.

"What do you want?"

"Aren't you going to introduce me to your Father Confessor?" she asked with a pout, her eyes still glued to Willi.

"You spied on me!"

"No, I didn't." Then ever so smoothly she stuck out her butt and shifted it sideways toward Willi and sat it down on the bench as though it had a life of its own. Willi watched in awe as he moved over to make room for her. Not a lot of room, I noticed. "You must be Inge," he spluttered, his cheeks turning bright red.

"What do you want?" I demanded to know.

"I don't want anything. I just wanted to come inside. It's cold out there. And then I saw you two sitting here. But I guess I better sit somewhere else." She got up like someone who expects to be called back, then said with a childish pout: "I know where I'm not wanted."

"Oh, you can stay. We don't mind, do we Stef?" Willi looked toward me as he said it, then turned back to Inge without waiting for my reply. I could have kicked him. And I could have kicked myself for wanting to kick Willi. And I could have kicked Inge for ruining everything.

Inge started a monologue that would not quit. I was beginning to feel like the fifth wheel on a wagon, and a very mismatched one at that. I wanted to leave in a dramatic huff, but I feared that Willi would be too busy staring at Inge to notice. And I most certainly would not clear the field for Inge, that egotistical brat. She had doused herself with perfume, but I smelled a rat. And there was that something about her face again...

I stayed and fumed. Inge jabbered on and acted stupid till the last minute. Angry, jealous, worried sick, I marched back to the convent with what seemed like the world on my shoulders. Inge traipsed behind, yelling, "wait up!" With her mouth going out of control the way it did from time to time, she was sure to trash my sacred secret. To prevent it, I was tempted to play up to her, but I couldn't bring myself to do it.

Upset with Willi, angry with Inge—my pit of misery was dug a little deeper by a letter from Mother in which she admonished me to get up my grades so that I could be an asset to Father's business after graduation. To have them plan my future for me without any input from me was bearable. But the thought of leaving Venusbrunn, leaving Willi, and not having any hope of seeing him again was enough to make me want to never get out of bed again.

But I got tired of hurting. I decided there was no point in making life more miserable than it already was. Inge was not to blame for being beautiful and thereby turning every guy's head. And I should be able to trust Willi to have more character than to get hooked by a pretty face. After all, he liked me! He liked the way I said whatever I thought, and he liked my brown eyes, and he thought my long braids were really neat. Counting my assets turned out to be a mistake.

The convent served as an old folks home for retired nuns. We never saw them except in the chapel where they sat huddled together in the back pews, rosary in hand, still and silent like shadows of the past. And like shadows they would suddenly fade away, one by one, without a word or commotion of any sort. That's how it was when Sister Cecelia died. We only knew that she was gone because we were told to attend her funeral.

"It's cold out there!" Inge protested.

"Then make sure that you dress properly," Sister Angela said with her usual waxy smile. "Frostbitten legs don't look very stylish," she added with a smirk.

"I am not going to stand out there in the snow for some stupid old nun that I don't even know!"

"We are all going. It's our Christian duty," Sister Angela said firmly, and the waxy smile vanished from her face.

"I'm not going, and they can't make me," Inge said, folded her arms across her chest and leaned back, like a tent peg, against the direction of pull.

"Oh, don't be such a baby," Gusti said.

"Hey! My parents aren't paying good money to have me freeze my butt off in the cemetery."

"So you forget the nylons and wear warm stockings," Roswitha suggested.

"And look like an old widow? Are you kidding?"

"Oh, don't make such a big deal out of it," Mechtild said. "It isn't going to kill you to help bury an old nun. It might even do you some good."

"And just what kind of wonderful benefit could I possibly gain from going to a funeral?" snippy Inge asked with her eyes rolled skyward.

"You might learn to think of something other than yourself."

Inge stuck her nose in the air and didn't reply.

It was Friday evening before I found out that the funeral would be on Saturday. Willi time! And I had waited all week! All week, I had waited to look into Willi's eyes, to see there that he still liked me. There was a lump in my throat every time I thought about him. The songs we had talked about kept haunting me. They would suddenly pop up in my mind, during study time, or in chapel, or during any unguarded, quiet moment. Then tears would rise in my eyes and send me to the toilet room to hide.

It turned out to be a long, cold winter. I didn't see Willi that week, and Willi didn't show up the following two weeks. Lotte, my friend from town whose brother was good friends with Willi, told me that Willi had been sick again. Then nobody was allowed downtown for a few weeks because a couple of boys had been seen on the convent grounds and - oh horrors - even inside the Villa. How they got there, what they were doing there, or whom they came to see, I never found out. Then Easter came, and we all went home for vacation.

On May Day, unofficial national hiking day, our entire school, boarding students and girls from town, went for a day-long hike to the old fortress ruin of Wildenburg. Sister Elisabeth lead the way, surrounded by the energetic ones who loved to walk and had no trouble keeping up with her. Sister Irmengard walked nearer the rear, encased by a group of fans, most prominent among them Helga who never left Sister's side. Our backpacks were filled with sandwiches, drinks, raincoats and umbrellas. Singing hiking songs while marching in rhythm, we followed the road South out of town for the first few miles and then took a hiking trail into the woods.

As usual, I brought up the rear where I could walk at my own pace, no one to crowd me in front and back. I could stop and watch the cute antics of the little wood mice without somebody going into hysterics. I could listen for woodpeckers hammering at trees and wonder why it sounded as if giants were wringing out trees the way I wrung out the laundry. I could stop to admire spider webs trimmed in dewdrop-pearls without somebody making fun of me.

The others had already reached the top of the hill that was covered in dense underbrush, huge firs, ash, beech, and maple trees. I had fallen ever farther behind till I could no longer see anyone. Suddenly, a loud hummm came zig-zagging around my head. I dodged the monstrous bug like a boxer when a wonderfully familiar voice called out: "It's a hummingbird."

I turned around, and there was Willi. He stepped out of the underbrush like an enchanted prince out of his animal hide. In my astonishment I didn't know what to say, just pointed up the trail in the direction of the others.

"They're at the top. They won't see us," Willi said with a sweet smile. Then he took my hand and pulled me gently into the underbrush from where he had come. He had spread his coat on the ground and pulled me down beside him, and my eyes started filling with tears.

"Lotte's brother told me. I took my bike and followed the road. It leads all the way to the top, but it's a lot longer than this hiking trail."

"Where is it now?"

"I hid it near the ruin. I know this place well. I've been here lots of times." And after studying my face for a moment, he said gently: "You look like you're going to cry." The tears that I had just barely managed to keep inside welled over and ran down my face.

Willi pulled out his handkerchief and dabbed at my tears and his gesture was so sweet that I cried even more.

"It's been a long time, I know," he said. He waited for me to calm down.

"I don't know why I'm acting so stupid."

"You're not acting stupid."

"Then why do I cry when there's nothing to cry about?"

"If you cry, there's a reason."

"What's the reason?"

"I don't know. But remember what you said in Cafe Pole one time?"

"I said a lot," I replied with some embarrassment, knowing full well that a willing ear could get me carried away.

"I mean the time when you said that it seemed like there are two of you, remember?"

"Oh yeah. The outer me and the inner me who does stupid stuff."

"There really is an inner person, you know. We all have it. And yours is very perceptive. It knows things that your outer person doesn't know."

"So why am I crying?"

"Your inner person could be sad about something."

"Like what?"

"I don't know," Willi said. His voice had become soft as a whisper. He was sitting with his chin propped on his raised knees and his arms slung around them, staring to the forest floor. And for an instant I felt as though he wanted me to know something but couldn't bring himself to tell me.

There was a call in the distance. On listening more carefully, I could make out my name. "Good grief! I gotta go!" I yelled and jumped up and Willi did likewise. "Cafe Pole? Saturday?" he asked.

"I'll be there!" Just before dashing off, I asked, " did you come just to see me?"

Willi nodded, and the light in his eyes was brighter than I had ever seen it before. I felt so light and happy that I kissed him on the cheek before racing up the trail.

"Don't step on any trolls!" he called softly.

I raced up the trail and found Inge looking for me. She gave me a long, suspicious look. "What are you doing?" she asked.

"I was watching hummingbirds," I said, trying hard to tone down the happiness that was doing funny things in my throat.

She still looked puzzled, so I added, "oh, you should see them. They are the cutest little things, and they zip around like big bugs, and they flap their little wings so fast that you can't see them." I went on and on with this

141

corny stuff till Inge gave up in disgust. Sister Irmengard, faithful Helga by her side, came toward me. "We thought you were lost," she said with a ready laugh that contradicted any concerns she might have had.

Still elated from seeing Willi I ventured into the area of the ruin that was called the Pallas and was once the living room of the Herren von Durne. The only recognizable item among crumbled stone walls was a huge fireplace that had served as the only source of heat, and beside the fireplace was one complete arched window set in a four foot thick wall. I stood in awe before the great fireplace, measuring its size with my eyes, my feet upon the stone floor where the Herren von Durne had once played host to the great poet Wolfram von Eschenbach, and I was overcome with the sensation of loss again.

I stood quietly, searching my mind, my feelings, my spirit for an answer to the question "what?" Any moment now, it seemed to me, I would have an answer, if I could just hold onto the feeling long enough.

"Come on, lets climb the tower," Inge said and nudged me, yanking me out of my explorations. When I tried to recapture the feeling, I could not. With a heavy sigh I followed her to the tower. It was the only part of the fortress that had not been dismantled over the centuries by area farmers who had come to look on the ruin as a rock quarry, that provided convenient building materials. An old man from the historical society had unlocked the heavy wooden door for us with a gigantic old key. "Slowly, girls," he admonished. "Careful! Watch yourselves."

The worn stone steps led in circular fashion to the top. Ever so often, narrow slits in the walls allowed a bit of light to shine on the dank darkness. We kept close to the walls where the steps were deepest and a thin handrail provided some safety.

Once we got out onto the platform and had adjusted to the light, the view was magnificent. The surrounding hills were covered with endless forests and were dotted by an occasional farm set in the mottled greens of surrounding fields and meadows. The fringes of Venusbrunn were visible in the valley. Patches of yellow gorse outlined the road we had hiked. Now and then, a car became visible on the road as it emerged from the trees. A single bicycle rider made his way along the road toward Venusbrunn.

Coming down, it was time for lunch. Inge and I sat together on the deep window ledge. When we were finished, we stood up in the arch, searching the distance for Venusbrunn. I imagined Willi, my knight in shining armor, riding home through the woods, across the moat, over the drawbridge, into the yard....

"Woods and forests I do not like; their dankness and darkness give me a fright," Inge mumbled, standing beside me in the arch. She stood so close to the outer edge that I got dizzy just looking at her. It must have been a good twenty-foot drop, straight down, and then some more down the hillside.

"Inge, get back. You're going to fall," I begged her.

"Who cares," she mumbled indifferently. She stood and stared and was so quiet that I knew something must be wrong.

"You don't care if you fall?"

"Not really."

"Is something the matter?" I asked.

She didn't answer right away. Then she said, slowly, thoughtfully, "why should anybody care if I'm dead or alive."

I waited a moment to see if anything more normal would follow. When nothing did, I began to feel very uneasy. I sat down and tugged on her skirt to get her to sit beside me. "You mean, you don't care if you live or die?" I asked.

"No. Sometimes, I think it's better to be dead. Then there's peace."

"Peace of what?"

"Just peace. And quiet."

Mechtild and Marlies had come nearby and heard Inge's last words. Mechtild jeered, "Inge wants peace. And quiet! Inge, who can rattle on like a long-distance freight train, wants quiet! That's hilarious." She laughed uproariously and, true to form, Marlies chimed in. Inge turned toward them, and the evil frown on her face quickly wiped the grin off mine.

"Shut up, you stupid cow," Inge growled. She turned back to face the woods. We sat quietly, legs dangling outside the window. I watched cloud shadows drift across the valley, the slopes and hills and endless woods, and I wondered if the Herren von Durne and their daughters had ever watched cloud shadows drift across their beautiful land. And surely, the poet Wolfram von Eschenbach had stood at this window and loved what he saw. When the silence had lasted long enough, I prodded, "are you gonna tell me what this is all about, or do you plan to take this mystery to the grave."

"Some day," she said softly. Then, with more conviction, "some day I'll tell you."

During May, which is dedicated to the Virgin Mary, we had prayer services in the Chapel every evening. Sister Irmengard had taught us some very beautiful songs, and sometimes, Helga who had a pretty voice and was Sister Irmengard's favorite - or perhaps it was the other way around - sang at night prayer.

On balmy evenings the windows of the Chapel stood wide open. The air was fresh then, not heavy as in the winter when the stagnant odors of the nuns' black habits filled the chapel and made me fidget with nausea. With the windows open, bird songs wafted in on the breeze and mixed with the fragrance of flowers and burning candles; it created a mood that was heavy with longing. Even Inge was not immune to it; she often stayed after prayers were over. She had become quieter, more serious since our hiking day to the ancient fortress. And sometimes, in the chapel, or in bed, or on a bench in the park, when she thought no one was watching, she cried.

Marlies was talking about her dead brother again, one evening. It seemed to me that he became ever more grand and wonderful in her memory, and that she grew in self-importance by virtue of having such a grand and wonderful brother. At first, Inge said nothing to all that sentimental gibberish. It wasn't out of respect, though, I could tell. She shifted around in her chair as if she wanted to do something and not do it, or say something and not say it. Then, as if she couldn't take it any more, she began to scoff at everything that Marlies said about her brother

"Why are you doing that?" Gusti finally demanded.

"Do what?"

"Badmouth everything she says, that's what."

"Because she's feeding us a lot of garbage. Brothers aren't like that," Inge replied, and the aggressive tone in her voice was alarming.

"Like what?" Roswitha asked innocently.

"All lovy-dovy, that's what."

"How would you know? You don't even have a brother," Mechtild challenged.

"I do, too!" Inge yelled and stood up. She did it with such vigor that her chair fell over. Then she ran out the door.

We looked at each other, puzzled, but since Inge's behavior had been annoying often enough we didn't mind her sudden exit.

Aha, I thought! The subject of brothers had upset her again. Maybe it was time to do something.

I couldn't find her in the toilet room, so she had to be in the park, the only other private place in the entire convent that wasn't locked up. I found her sitting on a bench under a trio of great fir trees. She was crying, crying so hard that her entire body shook. She didn't notice me till I sat down beside her.

"Want to talk about it?" I asked gently.

"I can't," Inge said, still sobbing, rocking back and forth as if in great pain. I waited. After she had calmed down a little she looked at me. Her eyes were still filled with tears, but her mouth was smiling as if with apology. Suddenly, it hit me!

"Now I know," I said triumphantly.

"Know what?"

"I know what's been bugging me about your face."

"What are you talking about?"

"I kept noticing something about your face, but I never knew what it was."

"What is it?"

"Even when you're smiling your eyes are always sad."

For a moment, Inge just stared at me with a blank expression while her mind processed what I had said. Then her face came alive. Inge understood. Her lips clenched shut, and the corners of her mouth drooped, and her forehead wrinkled up in pain and the tears flowed again.

I was startled at her reaction. I had always wished that people would pay attention to what I say, but this reaction was awesome. Then I remembered Mother Superior saying that Inge had had some trouble in her life.

"You have to talk about it," I said firmly. "It's the only way to get rid of the problem."

"It will never go away," Inge said between blowing and sniffling and wiping eyes and nose.

"Is that why you wish you were dead?"

Inge nodded.

"Well, you're not dead, and you're not going to die, so the only thing to do is to get rid of this thing by talking it out. It has to do with brothers, doesn't it?"

146

Inge nodded. Then slowly, haltingly, she began to talk about her older brother, Herbert, who no longer lived at home. He had been sent to an institution for young offenders.

"Why? What did he do?"

"Ever since I was ten, he.... he...." The words died in her tear-choked voice. It made me shiver with dread.

"What did he do?" I asked timidly.

Stiff and tense, Inge was rocking back and forth, her hands tucked between her knees as if she were trying to keep herself from falling apart. I began to wonder if it might not be better to keep the dreadful secret under wraps. But I sensed that dragging it out into the open was the better thing to do—like sweeping up dirt, looking at it, seeing it, knowing it for what it is before it can be gotten rid off.

"Did he... molest you?"

Tear-choked Inge could only nod. I felt so bad that I put my arm around her. Like a drowning man, Inge clung to me and sobbed uncontrollably.

"All right, what happened?" Willi asked. Before I had said a word, he knew that something was bothering me. I frowned at him with pretended annoyance for knowing me so well. "Your face is an open book," he explained and laughed.

"Okay, okay. Inge told me something bad."

"What did Inge tell you?" Willi said, and with a broad, sweet smile he laid his crossed arms before him on the table and leaned forward so as not to miss a word. I wondered if he showed a little too much interest.

"She told me that her brother, ever since she was ten years old, her brother..." To my surprise, I had trouble saying the word. I felt embarrassed before Willi. I gave myself an inner shove and came out with it: "....molested her."

147

"Oh God, that's awful!"

"I think that's why Inge's been acting so stupid at times. Trying to keep it all inside, you know. Must be dreadful to carry around such a secret."

"Her parents didn't know?"

"Her brother threatened to kill her if she said anything."

"Oh, the poor thing. How is she dealing with it?"

"I don't know. Eventually, her brother got found out and was sent away, but her parents never did anything for her. Oh yeah, they took her on a fancy trip to Rome, Italy. They must think that a visit to the Pope is great therapy. But they never talk about what her brother did to her."

"They ought to castrate a guy who does that."

We sat quietly, nibbling on our goodies, trying to digest the horror that had been done to Inge. But the silence became awkward. Willi said something, I said something, unimportant things, silly things. Willi seemed preoccupied with his thoughts. Finally, he saidm "if Inge understood that rape violates the body, not the Spirit, it might help her."

"What do you mean? How would it help her?"

"Well, if she didn't identified with her body...."

"What the heck are you saying? "

"I'm saying that we are not our bodies," Willi said slowly. "We are Spirit, see?"

"You mean the soul that never dies?"

"Something like that."

"So?"

"So, you, Stephanie, are a Spirit, and your body is only a coat that you wear for this time on earth. Eventually, the coat wears out. That's when you die. The real Stephanie is Spirit, and Spirit cannot be hurt. You see? And if you know, really know and understand that you are Spirit, then you can better survive an attack on the body, get it?"

"Then it's more like an attack on the coat, instead of on the person?"

"That's the idea."

"And the person is really Spirit, not flesh?"

"That's right. And Spirit cannot be hurt."

"Well, yeah, I see what you mean. But... you can't just take off your body and hang it in the closet. How do you separate yourself from it?"

"By shifting your consciousness to Spirit."

"Good grief! That sounds pretty complicated."

"Not really. You actually do it all the time."

"I do?"

"Sure. Want to do a little experiment?"

"You mean right here? Right now?"

"Why not."

"All right. If you think so." Might even be fun, I thought, and definitely different from anything else I had ever done.

"Do you have a dog, or cat?"

"No. But I had a little calf of my own on my grandpa's farm."

"OKAY then," Willi said. "Close your eyes and make an image of that calf in your mind. Paint a picture of it," he added, seeing the puzzled look on my face.

I did. And when I saw the little animal in my mind I stroked its coarse fur, and scratched its curly forehead, and felt the velvety softness of the ears and the hard knobby areas where horns would grow.

"What are you doing?" Willi asked.

"I'm feeling the calf's fur, and its soft ears, and the hard place on its head," I said.

"There! You've done it," Willi said.

"What did I do?"

"You shifted your consciousness to the calf."

"I did? It's that easy?"

149

"With things you know, sure. But it's harder with Spirit, because we don't really know Spirit very well. We identify with our bodies too much. But you get the idea, right?"

"That's fantastic! I mean, I could actually, really feel those soft velvety ears, as if I had them right here in my hand!"

"Isn't it great! You can do that in all sorts of situations." He smiled mischievously. "For instance, any time you want to, you can be with me. You just close your eyes, and form an image of me in your mind, and concentrate on it, and presto..."

"Where did you learn all that?" I asked with awe at such exulted knowledge.

"My Mom. She's clairvoyant, too, you know. She taught me a lot."

"Does she know about me?"

"Oh yes. I tell her most everything. She doesn't mind. She says the nuns keep you girls on too short a leash. It's unnatural."

"Gee, my mother should take lessons from your mother. But say, could this thing about consciousness help Inge?"

"Sure. It's a type of meditation. It's good for anybody."

An extraordinary thought entered my mind. It felt quite odd and unfamiliar. I tossed it about while I sipped on my apple juice. I tossed it about, put it down, picked it up again.

"What are you thinking?" Willi asked.

"I'm thinking," I said slowly, weighing the possible consequences of what I was about to propose. "I'm thinking that you should explain it to Inge. Maybe I'll bring her along some Saturday." I watched Willi's face closely. It lit up a little, but I couldn't tell if it was from the thought of helping someone in need or from the prospect of seeing gorgeous Inge again. Then, a worried look spread over his face as he said, "I don't know. I can't believe she'd want to talk to me. I'm practically a stranger."

"Well, she wouldn't have to tell you what happened to her. You could just explain this thing about not identifying with the body."

"That's true. Still... I don't think I could discuss such powerful stuff with just anybody. You're interested, so that's okay. But most people aren't. She'll think I'm weird and then it won't do any good what I say. Not that it matters what she thinks. But if she really wants to - all right."

For days, the ups and downs of indecisiveness jerked me about. One minute I planned to be gracious and take Inge to Willi to be enlightened; the next minute, fear of the consequences made me change my mind. Then I told myself that Inge's emotional state was not my concern. I was not responsible for solving her problems. And I most certainly was not obliged to share my boyfriend with her.

But my inner person kept nagging me, accusing me, shaming me for not trusting Willi. Finally, one night, still wrestling with myself, I resolved to help Inge and take her to Willi. With that settled, I rolled over to sleep, but sleep was slow in coming. And then, in the space between waking and sleeping, something made me cry again.

I was going to be Inge's Savior. I was going to do something that was very selfless and compassionate. Downright noble, it was. But Inge didn't want to. "I don't want anybody to know. That goes double for guys!" she said.

"But he can help you," I insisted

"Nobody can help me," Inge said stoically. "And don't you dare tell anybody about this."

Concentrating on bookkeeping became difficult with Inge's problems and the planned rescue on my mind.

Sister Harmony seemed to know right away that I was preoccupied. Maybe the drop to D in my test had something to do with it. "It looks like you didn't have a chance to copy from anyone this time," she said with her squishy soft lips pulled into an oily smile.

"I don't copy," I protested.

"Of course not. You just suddenly forgot everything you had learned," she said with mock sincerity. "Remember, your parents want me to report to them."

Great! That was all I needed. Mother firmly believed that priests and nuns are God's deputies on earth. Since God is infallible, so must be his deputies. My parents would take Sister Harmony's word over mine any time. Not that they would ever ask for mine!

Studying didn't get any easier with the heat wave bearing down on us toward the middle of June. It hadn't rained for two weeks. Once in a great while, a single cloud shuffled across the sun, but that was all it did. "Yeah, just wait till July, when school's out. That's when it'll start raining," Mechtild quipped.

"And you lie there by the swimming pool in your wet swim suit and freeze to death," Marlies added.

"I always take an extra blanket along, to wrap myself in," Helga added.

I would have relished lying by the pool any which way, but no such luck would be waiting for me who owned too many little sisters and brothers. They would have to go to the rest room, or they wanted an ice cream cone from the pool Cafe, had lost the badminton birdie or wanted to play by the nearby river.

"The only place to get any real sun is in Italy," Inge said with great authority.

"Oh no! You're not going to brag about Italy again," Mechtild wailed and slammed her hands over her ears. Inge sent her an evil frown.

"Are your parents going to take you to Rome again?" Roswitha asked.

"I don't know yet," Inge replied. Then, drawing out the words in sing-songy rhythm, she added, "could be Italy, could be Spain. Just anywhere there's no rain."

"Oh, you're so clever with words," Marlies sneered. Inge turned away and left the room.

"I think you hurt her feelings," I said.

"So what! She hurts my feelings all the time."

"Just what does she do that hurts your feelings?"

"She talks!" Marlies said and laughed uproariously. Some of the others chimed in.

"Come on now. Don't be like that. She's miserable enough without us making her feel worse," I said.

"Why, what's the matter with her?" Gusti asked.

"I can't talk about it. I gave her my word." I wished I had never said it because now, Mechtild, Marlies, Ellen, and even Helga kept nagging me to tell what the trouble was.

"She gave her word, so leave her alone," Gusti finally said.

The evening was warm and fragrant; we said night prayers in the park by the little stone grotto of the Virgin Mary. Someone had brushed the spider webs from the statue and placed flowers at the Virgin's feet. Sister Irmengard asked Helga to sing a favorite song. And Helga sang an emotional love song to the Virgin Mary. Her reddish blond hair lay in orderly curls around her broad face, its fair skin stained by clumps of irregular freckles. Her voice rang clear and jubilant in the soft, still dusk.

As the pink blush of the Western sky faded away I felt a deep yearning for Willi and I ached with loneliness. Doubts and suspicions haunted me again, doubts about Inge meeting with Willi. It was as if I knew I was headed toward something bad but could not stop myself; as if facing the approaching bad thing was something I had to endure, and the sooner it happened the sooner I could put it behind me.

On Saturday, I said to Inge, "come with me to Cafe Pole."

"And do what?"

"Willi can explain something to you that'll help you to deal with.... you know what."

"You didn't tell him, did you?"

"No," I lied.

"Well, for your information, I'm dealing just fine with my problem; so just mind your own business," she said, rather snippy. The thought occurred to me that she might be sorry for having revealed her most secret and private problem. Perhaps she'd rather forget she ever talked about it. But I pressed on, "he can explain something to you that's really interesting. For anybody, actually."

"What can he explain to me?"

"Well about the body, and the Spirit, and how this is just a coat we're wearing—I can't say it right."

"Are you sure you want me there? With your Willi?" she quipped half serious, half teasing.

"It's alright," I relented, faking confidence while I studied her flawless complexion and her platinum blond curls and her gorgeous figure and her perfect everything. Something inside me demanded an examination of my mental faculties; something else tried to calm me with the notion that whatever would happen was meant to be.

"Okay, but I'll make no promises. If I don't feel like talking I won't."

"That's fine with me."

We were headed for the front door when Sister Filikula, the cleaning nun, grabbed me by the arm. She was low in status and short in stature, but she had a surprisingly powerful grip. With a smile that foreclosed any objections she said that she needed someone to wash the upper windows because they were too high for her. I was just the

154

right size for the job, she claimed as if it were a great honor to be chosen by her.

"But I was just on my way to confession," I lied.

"You can go next week," she replied sweetly and firmly.

"But I'm not the only tall one around."

"Oh, you'll do just fine."

"But... but..." I looked toward Inge, my eyes pleading with her to come up with an idea. But she had none. Sister Filikula dragged me to the classroom, waving Inge off. I could see a slight grin on her flawless face just before she turned to leave, her head held high, her platinum blond curls bouncing confidently, and her hips swinging seductively in her clingy red dress.

"What did he say? What did he say?" I practically fell all over Inge when she finally got back at coffee time. It was devastating to realize that the state of my happiness depended on words from Inge's mouth. But the dining hall was full of girls. Sister Angela did guard duty and Sister Fallada was present for reinforcement. The coming graduation was causing excitement and extra work. Sister Irmengard showed up from time to time to take some of us to the piano room to rehearse our singing parts for the graduation performance. She had chosen Friedrich Schiller's very long poem, "The Bell," of which some parts would be recited, some were solos or duos, and some were choruses.

Except for a few whispered words across the table, there was no way to talk with Inge. I couldn't help staring at her face, her body, watching her every move, as if looking hard enough would reveal some little clue about what had taken place between her and Willi. She seemed to relish my misery and took her sweet time eating. She didn't finish until the bell rang for study time.

Once in the classroom, Sister Irmengard came to fetch Helga and me to practice our parts. When we got back, Sister Harmony drilled Inge and Gusti in their recitations. Finally, toward the end of study period, Inge agreed to talk to me in the toilet room. She had gone to see Willi and told him that I couldn't come. Then she had gone to the library to read.

"That's it?" I asked.

"That's it," she said with a slight smile of satisfaction.

"You went to the library to read?"

"Why not," Inge said, getting resentful. I hastened to assure her that I didn't mean anything by it.

"But what did he say when he heard that I wasn't coming?"

"That it was too bad."

"How long did you stay with him? Did you talk about anything? How did he look when you said I couldn't come? Did he look sad?" I just had to get something more out of her. But there was nothing else, or rather, Inge claimed that there was nothing else.

"Did he say he was going to be at the Cafe next Saturday? He must have said more than just 'that's too bad.' What else did he say?"

"Oh, leave me alone," Inge yelled, went out and slammed the door.

I spent a week in utter misery because Inge avoided me. All my efforts to keep my wobbly confidence intact were in vain. It was painful to have Inge right under my nose all day, reminding me that she had seen Willi, had talked with him, had been sitting with him. She was the only one who knew what had happened on that last Saturday in June.

Willi didn't come to Cafe Pole on the following Saturday, neither did he show the week after that. Lotte, who could have given me news of Willi, had left with her family for a vacation in Spain.

The last days of my tenth grade year passed in a fog, a thick, ugly fog of doubt and suspicion and jealousy. Only the practice sessions with Sister Irmengard provided some relief from the unbearable pain. To save myself, I stopped thinking about Willi. To keep tears from embarrassing me, I stopped caring about anything. I sat and studied, walked and studied, talked and studied, anything to keep from thinking about what caused me pain. And if there was no one around to talk to I talked to myself.

To make matters worse, during the last week of school a feeling of urgency came over me, of foreboding, as though my best friend had moved to the other side of the world without saying goodbye, never to return. It created an inner restless muddle that was eased only by the stepped-up activities of the coming graduation.

Our parents were invited to the performance on the last day of school, a Friday. The movable wall between dining room and classroom was opened to allow for a stage-like platform to be erected. A large retractable curtain was hung before the stage and chairs were set up in the classroom for the audience.

The performance began at nine o'clock, but my parents had not yet arrived. It didn't matter much; the emotional fog that surrounded me had dulled my awareness of the outside. Restless and confused, I felt an inner pressure that made me want to do something, only I didn't know what.

The performance began with one of the girls from town reciting a prologue, which was followed by a chorus... my parents will take me home soon after the performance...a duo...I'll never see Willi again...my parents walked in...I've got to talk to Willi before I leave...a recitation...I've got to see him before I leave...my solo...how do I get to Willi?...I opened my mouth and the words came out... could run to his house right after the performance...a chorus...that's what I'll do...

I knew that my parents would want to have polite chit-chats with the nuns. As soon as the performance was over, and before they had a chance to come looking for me, I ran to Willi's house. I knew where he lived. Lotte had shown it to me.

The closer I got to Willi's house, though, the weirder I felt. What on earth was I going to do there? Ask to see him? What if he wasn't home? What if his mother opened the door? Or his father! What if he was there, but he didn't want to see me? What if his eyes were dark and his smile was cold?

When I got to the house, I lost my nerve. I walked past it and turned into the next side street, turned again at the next corner, turned again at the next corner, walked in circles around the block. When I got up the courage to ring the bell, my hands were shaking.

A tall woman answered the door, and I felt as if I was looking at Willi, only female and older. Her hair was short and wavy, her expression quite somber. My feeling of urgency got so strong that I could hardly make myself understood when I asked for Willi.

"Are you Stephanie?" she asked with a kind smile.

"Yes. How did you know?"

"Willi described you to me. Come in," she said, closed the apartment door and motioned me into the living room to her right.

"Is he at home?"

"Are you coming from the convent?" she asked.

"Yes. Is Willi home? Can I talk to him?"

She invited me to sit with her on the sofa. Her face looked tired, and her eyes were sad. That's when I noticed that her clothes and stockings were all black. It reminded me of the old widows who go to mass every day, who wear black all the time because a new death has occurred before the last mourning year is over. And then, as if the final piece of the puzzle had just fallen into place, I suddenly knew what Spirit had known all along. "Willi died, didn't he?" I managed to say as I watched her face carefully. She was not startled by what I said, did not refute it, did not look at me with astonishment and ask how I could possibly have come up with such a monstrous idea.

"Yes, honey, he did," Willi's mother said, and her hands fiddled with a large handkerchief.

I could feel numbness spreading through my body as I sat and stared at the floor that was covered by a carpet with geometric design, and I studied its color, and pattern, and shape...

She told me that Willi had had a kidney infection a few summers ago, and that he had never totally recovered from it. His kidneys had grown weaker and more susceptible, and the last bout with infection had been too much for him.

"When did he... When did it happen?"

"It was on a Monday at the End of June."

"So he couldn't have been at Cafe Pole on the last Saturday in June?"

"No, he was much too sick."

"I didn't even get to say good-bye," is all I managed to say. Then I realized that there were no tears in my eyes, and I wondered why.

"Willi wants me to tell you that you mustn't be sad. He's still around, you know. We just can't see him anymore."

If that was meant to make me feel better, it didn't work. What good would it do to know Willi was around but not to be able to look into his eyes and see there the beauty that gave meaning to my life. No more smiles to make me feel happy, no more deep talk to feed my mind, no one who cared about my feelings...

Still numb and not knowing what to say or do, I got up to leave. "Wait, I have something for you," Willi's mother said. "Willi asked me to give it to you. I would have mailed it to your home if you hadn't come. He wanted to give it to you personally, but when he didn't recover..." She turned away, went to a drawer and pulled out a small box that was wrapped in gift paper. "Open it," she said with an encouraging smile.

"What is it?" I asked the way people do to bridge an awkward silence. Underneath the wrapping paper I found a little jewelry box. Inside the box lay a heart-shaped locket. It had a photo of me in one side and a photo of Willi in the other side. A tiny card was enclosed, and on it, Willi had written something in small, meticulous print. I could barely make it out through the tears that were filling my eyes - Reach out with your mind and you will find me.

Epilogue

Years later, when the mysterious sensations that I had felt in Venusbrunn had not faded but rather grown stronger, I visited Willi's mother. I wanted to ask her that one question I hadn't thought to ask because Willi's death had wiped it from my mind: had I ever been in Venusbrunn before?

The moment my eyes took hold of her face, Willi's image flashed through my mind and I felt a sting of loneliness and sadness. Willi's mother was no longer wearing black; she wore bright colors and seemed hardly any older than the first and last time I had seen her. She recognized me right away, even remembered my name. She invited me inside. We sat just where we had been sitting on that dreadful day of graduation.

"Willi used to tell me about you and all the things you know," I said. "Do you know if I have ever been in Venusbrunn before I came to school here? I've had this sensation for years, and it just won't give me any peace. You know what I mean?"

Willi's mother nodded. "To know ourselves is important. And the more we know, and the deeper and clearer we can see inside ourselves, the better for us. If the need to know haunts you then it's a sure sign that you're ready to know."

"So... have I ever been here before? Before I came to school here?" I felt tense, excited, as if confirmation of my very being hung in the balance.

"Yes you have."

Suddenly, I knew. I knew that deep down inside I had always known it. I had known it when I first heard the name Venusbrunn, in the back of the park, at the old mill, the fortress ruin...

"How did I know it?"

"Because you are sensitive to the influence of the Spirit, and Spirit knows everything. Now that you know consciously, you can better cooperate with the guidance of Spirit. And when you do that, you can never go wrong."

"One more thing: Willi said once that we might have been together in a previous life. I'd like to think that it's true. Is it?"

"Yes. And Willi knew it. We often talked about it."

"Why didn't he tell me that he knew it?"

"Because you weren't ready for it then. Now you are, that's why you came back. And now you can know that many of your lives emanated from Venusbrunn. Some you lived as a man, some as a woman. You and Willi were together more than once but in different roles, as siblings, friends, even lovers. And if you're both willing and find it useful for your further evolution you will be together again."

Additional books by Rita Traut Kabeto

Call from the Past is the first book of a trilogy that includes
Fanny's Flight and
Dagobert
None of the usual genres fit my writings so I came up with a new one:
Metaphysically spiced autobiographical fiction.

Crows and other Pedestrians is a collection of personal, critical and historical essays, some fun crow poetry, a couple of riddles, a short story and a travelogue to Weimar in the former East Germany just two years after the wall came down; it gives the reader a good look at life under Communism.
When the Blackbird called, a book of poetry

Run Away Jamie is a novel for the middle grades
How the Mouse Spoiled Everything, a chapter book for children with illustrations
Tales from Bohemia, a translation from German, a storybook about nature spirits and their interactions with humans.